Abuse of
Privilege

Abuse of Privilege

Milt Anderson

To order additional copies of this book, contact:
Xlibris Corporation
1-888-795-4274
www.Xlibris.com
Orders@Xlibris.com
22497

Dedication and Acknowledgements

First and foremost, I must thank my wife for her love and support throughout my endeavor in Seton Hill's *Master of Arts in Writing Popular Fiction* Program. I would also like to thank the students in the workshops and members of my critique groups who spent their time and expertise on my work. A special thanks to Cheryl Woods who was my critique partner from the start and provided invaluable technical knowledge and motivation. A special thanks to Seton Hill University and Dr.'s Lee McClain, Al Wendland and Mike Arnzen for making this program possible.

I would like to thank my mentors, Patrick Picciarelli, who started me off on the right path to writing this novel and Ed Dee who provided the refinement and guidance for its conclusion. I appreciate the technical advice of Carol Conte and the expertise of Kevin Iacovangelo and his staff at Right Byte Computer for keeping my computer functional and on line. Also, a special thanks to Anne Fotheringham for her much needed copyediting.

I would also like to thank Dr. Mike Danoff who volunteered to design the front cover. He coordinated with Kirk Salopek, a teacher at Thomas Jefferson High School, and Jeremy Goodman, the student who actually created the artwork.

I dedicate this book to the memory of George (Moldy) Rixey who provided the initial impetus for my interest in writing, to Patrick Picciarelli for recognizing that desire, and to my wife, Louise, for encouraging me to seize this opportunity.

Chapter 1

The '92 Bronco rode like a new vehicle; the hard rain and puddled road offered no resistance to the old man's car.

"Charlie took pretty good care of this old heap," Wally Gustafson said, trying to change the subject and calm J.C. down at the same time. "Rides like the fifty-six Merc I used to have. Solid."

J.C. Ducheck was silent. He glared ahead through the darkness and driving rain, looking for the answer that lay ahead, that would, for better or for worse, define his existence.

Wally turned in his seat, the seat belt shoulder restraint stopping him momentarily. "Look, don't get your hopes up. This may turn out to be a dud."

"I don't think so," J.C. said, breaking his gaze from the road. The muscles of his jaw flexed and determination seemed to shoot out of his ice-blue eyes. "Jason sounded pretty excited on the phone. He knows who's trying to kill him."

Wally rubbed the gray stubble on his chin. "I still think it's odd that he asked you to meet him at the Sit n' Bull. Why couldn't he tell you on the phone who this guy is? Why meet at a bar? A gay bar at that."

J.C. shrugged. "He's scared. Says he can't trust the police. Besides, he probably feels safe around his friends."

"Sounds like he's paranoid to me."

J.C. cracked a smile. He knew Wally understood the gravity of the situation and was trying to ease the tension. He felt a special kinship to Wally, who was like his uncle although J.C. was 10 years younger than Wally's actual nephew, Paul.

J.C. tuned the radio to a light jazz station. He liked jazz—didn't know why. Probably because of the soothing effect it had on him. J.C. could tell it had the same effect on Wally. His grip on the armrest eased and he turned his attention to the old neighborhood's architecture, no longer concerned with the road ahead.

J.C. became anxious as he turned off Pricedale Road onto Donner. The tract of land to the river was once occupied by a steel mill and surrounded by company homes and small businesses. The mill's pulsating orange and brilliant white lights that used to light up the sky were gone, but tomorrow would be different. The 4th of July fireworks would illuminate the sky with streaming rockets and explosive bursts of vibrant colors. Tonight, only the flitter of blue light that gave name to the Sit n' Bull Lounge remained.

The Bronco heaved from side to side and lurched front to rear like a stagecoach riding over a weather-beaten trail. J.C. thought it might be quicker to drive through the different buildings, but after looking at the rusted and swayback superstructures, he continued on the pockmarked road.

After the mill closed and people left, the housing fell to disrepair and the area was finally condemned. All but the Sit n' Bull. The redevelopment authority wanted the entire tract of land for a racetrack, but the bar refused to budge. The authority didn't want to pay what the bar wanted or use eminent domain as its closing would infuriate the gay community and reflect badly on public officials. So the politicians would slowly strangle the business—in a politically correct way—and take over the property without cost to the taxpayer.

J.C. had trouble staying on the road. The slow-moving wipers couldn't keep up with the downpour and the white, painted lines that had been on the road were long gone. The Southwest Pittsburgh and Lake Central Railroad crossing provided the only level, maintained section of the neglected road. But that lasted only a few seconds. Only occasional bursts of lightning kept the road in view and illuminated the once live structures that now stood like giant, fractured tombstones.

Wally pointed to three large rusted hulks off to the right. "Those are blast furnaces. They're obsolete now. Gave way to basic oxygen and electric furnaces." He paused. "At one time there were dozens of those old furnaces along this river," he gestured toward them proudly. "Won the war for us you know."

J.C. knew Wally had mixed emotions when he took an early retirement from Waltham Steel Company just five miles upstream. "You work on those furnaces at your mill?"

"Worked on everything. Pipefitters go where they're needed. There are thousands of miles of plumbing and pipes in a steel mill."

J.C. wanted to continue talking to Wally about his former job, but not right now. They were entering the Sit n' Bull's parking lot and he was eager to see Jason.

The blue neon sign perched on the roof above the entrance barely illuminated the parking lot. Only outlines of vehicles and reflections off cars' chrome and glass were visible due to a moonless sky and the drenching rain.

J.C. found a parking space in the second row. A clap of

thunder shook the ground as they got out of the Bronco. They rushed toward the bar, wind blowing their umbrellas inside out.

They paused under the roof's overhang trying to collapse their broken rain-gear. A Beatles' hit "You Really got a Hold on Me" vibrated through the thin walls.

The same blue light they had seen on the bar's sign plus the smell of alcohol and tobacco greeted them when J.C. opened the door.

J.C. and Wally walked in, shaking off the rain. They stood there, as if on an island surrounded by a sea of distrust, looking for Jason. Fingers were pointing and heads came together in whispers.

Wally started to sing when the second verse started. "I don't like you, but I love you."

It all started to look like a slow motion movie to J.C. The men at the bar turned to look at them as if seen through the flipping of flash cards, the stroboscopic black light slowed their movements even more. Even the music seemed to slow, but it glided on.

Embracing couples on the dance floor appeared to be dressed in flavors rather than colors. They looked comfortable in their surroundings, enjoying a freedom that they certainly did not have at their day jobs. The dancers' feet followed reflections on the floor from a mirrored sphere that hung above the center of the dance floor, creating the effect of a human merry-go-round.

J.C. walked to the bar keeping step with the music and found a vacant spot at the corner. He motioned for service. The young bartender had spiked, iridescent blue hair. He wore skin-tight black leather pants with matching vest—no shirt. His nose ring moved in sync with "What'll you have?"

Wally whispered in J.C.'s ear. "That kid looks like a prize chicken I saw at the county fair."

J.C. wiped the smile from his face and the remaining wetness from his brow. "Jason Saxberg asked us to meet him here."

Spike looked relived. "Oh . . . yeah. Jason," he said, scanning the dance floor. "I don't see him." He held up a finger. "Wait a minute, I'll check."

Wally leaned over J.C's shoulder and whispered, "Don't attempt to sit down."

"What? Why not?"

"Someone might offer to push your stool in for you."

J.C. stifled a laugh. He tried to focus on the bartender who was questioning patrons. J.C. watched as the succession of men being interviewed shrugged their shoulders and nodded their heads in a negative manner.

The bartender came back and looked at Wally with an admiring smile, one that insinuated that an old man struck it rich with such a good-looking young man. Wally stared at his hair.

"He's not here," Spike said, still smiling. Wally straightened his collar and smiled back.

"He said he'd meet us at ten o'clock," J.C. said, glancing at the patrons and then at clock on the wall behind the bar.

"Well I asked everyone," the bartender said, placing his hands on his hips, "and he's not here."

"What kind of car does he have?" Wally asked, seeing that J.C. was at a loss for words.

"A Dodge Colt. Red."

"Thanks," Wally said, grabbing J.C.'s arm. "We'll wait for him outside."

As they neared the door, the noise and activity level rose to its former, boisterous level.

The rain hadn't eased. They ran to the Bronco without opening their useless umbrellas—and got soaked. J.C. sat behind the wheel, dripping wet, wondering if this meeting was all wet too—maybe Jason Saxberg didn't know who was trying to kill him. But he had come all this way in a nasty storm. He'd involved Wally, who was just as determined as he was to find the truth. J.C. knew he had to stay, find Jason, and hear him out; it was crucial.

"My ass is wet," Wally said, squirming in his seat. "I think I'm catching cold." He uttered a fake cough. "Maybe it's something worse," His eyebrows rose as he turned toward J.C. "You know, from being in that bar."

Another lightning strike illuminated the area like a stadium during Monday Night Football.

The flash lasted long enough to give J.C. a glimpse of something red at the end of the parking lot, near Cross Creek. Jason Saxberg's car? It looked like a Dodge Colt.

J.C. started the engine and shifted into gear.

"Where you goin'? Aren't we waiting for Jason?"

J.C. pointed at a spot near the creek where the lightning flashed. "That looks like his car."

"Where?"

J.C. pulled out and headed in the direction of the red blur. He tried the high beams, but they were useless in the torrent. He switched to low.

The Dodge came into view.

"There it is," J.C. said. "Why didn't he go inside?"

J.C. pulled in back of the car. Before he shifted into park, Wally jumped out and headed for the passenger door.

"It's locked," he said, squinting as the rain pelted him full in the face.

As J.C. moved toward the driver's door, a dark pickup parked next to the Dodge started to drive off. As J.C. watched it leave, he stumbled over something. He fell, landing on his elbow and left side. As he turned to see what he had fallen over, a clap of thunder shook the ground and another flash of lightning revealed a body. J.C. inched closer and looked into the face of Jason Saxberg.

"Wally!"

Wally dashed around the car and stood silent, looking at the body's image fade in and out from Mother Nature's lightshow just as the black light stroboscope had bounced off dancers in the bar.

J.C. checked Jason's carotid artery for a pulse. "He's dead!" he shouted, getting up and running toward the Bronco. Wally followed his lead and jumped in at the same time as J.C.

"The killer's in that truck," J.C. said, starting the engine and then yanking the shifter into gear. "We've got to catch him!"

J.C. stomped on the accelerator. The wheels spun on the loose gravel and mud. The Bronco slid through the parking lot, narrowly missing cars. Wally gripped the armrest again.

The red taillights of the truck were barely visible, the headlights, though, shone into the downpour like a pair of spotlights, the beams bouncing up and down like the white dot above the televised words of Christmas carols.

Three, more intense beacons of light appeared to the right. A train had come around a bend and was approaching the crossing. The truck sped up, sliding and bouncing toward its only escape when it suddenly went off the road and stopped.

J.C. saw his opportunity; he was less than 100 yards away. "Looks like he got stuck in the mud."

"We got him now," Wally said, reaching to the small of his back and retrieving a .32 caliber pistol.

J.C. almost ran off the road. "Put that gun away! You're not going to shoot him!"

"I don't intend to," Wally said, caressing the firearm. "This is a negotiating tool. People listen to Mister Smith and Mister Wesson."

They were within forty yards of the truck when it inched its way out of the mud.

"Step on it J.C.; it's pulling loose!"

J.C. fought the wheel as he tried to stay on the road. He was closing the gap between them when the truck lurched onto the road and headed for the level crossing, swaying

15

and bouncing over the potholes. It was twenty yards from the crossing. The train braked but couldn't stop.

Wally pointed over the dashboard. "They're going to hit!"

The truck sprung forward, getting traction from the well-kept area around the crossing, then shot across the tracks inches in front of the locomotive.

J.C. slammed on the brakes; the Bronco slid to a stop less than five yards from the train. He pounded the steering wheel with his fist.

"He got away. The son of a bitch killed Jason and got away." J.C. slumped over the wheel and sobbed. "He's dead. Dead as any chance I had of finding out who I am."

Wally placed a comforting hand on his shoulder. They sat there, in the rain, watching the train's cars pass before them. J.C. knew that the identity of Jason's killer died with him, but what bothered him most was that he knew the man who killed Jason was the same man who was trying to kill him as well.

Chapter 2

"I can remember the first day of my life," J.C. said, wiping the bar in a wide, circular pattern. "It was August the twenty seventh, nineteen ninety-nine. The prior twenty odd years are a complete blank."

He was talking to the only customer in Ducheck's Bar, a young man named Russell, who was searching the city for his aunt.

"What's that, some kind of doubletalk?" Russell asked. "Is that a riddle or somethin'?"

J.C. knew how confusing his statement was. Many townspeople didn't understand his problem; some people looked at him strangely as if he was from another planet. Since he and Russell were alone, J.C. thought it would be a good time to talk about his situation, to see if a stranger might understand.

"The doctors called it the fugue—"

"Wasn't that a dance back in the seventies?"

"I don't know Russell. I mean, I can't remember. That's part of what I suffer from. It's called the Fugue State."

"Isn't that amnesia? And call me Nuggets. All my friends do."

"Okay . . . Nuggets. No, it's not about memory loss; it's about a complete personality change. Like becoming a new person."

Nuggets' eyebrows arched over his big brown eyes. "A personality change? How the hell can that happen?"

"It's very rare; some doctors haven't heard of it at all. In my case, a neurologist said it was due to a life-threatening experience." J.C. noticed the puzzled look on Nuggets' face, as if he had been asked a stupid question. "Someone tried to kill me. I was shot twice, once in the head, and left for dead."

J.C. heard the unmistakable metallic sound of the latch on the bar's oak front door open. Nuggets turned around and noticed a man in his fifties with curly gray hair standing in the doorway. He was wearing a gray t-shirt with a Claridge Casino logo silk-screened across his chest. His baggy blue jeans sagged over his blue, New Balance walking shoes.

Nuggets turned around and continued, "You were shot in the head!"

Wally walked up and slowly slid onto a stool next to Nuggets. He studied Nuggets' features starting from his short, curly dark hair to the spit-shined low-quarters on his feet.

Before J.C. could answer, Wally spoke up. "That's why he's so fucked up," he said. "Whoever the dumb son of a bitch was that shot him couldn't hit the side of a barn . . . from inside."

J.C. and Wally both laughed. Nuggets looked from one man to the other.

"Nuggets, this is Wally Gustafson," J.C. said, pouring a beer for Wally. "He's a good friend of mine. He was in the hospital room when I woke up that day."

Wally acknowledged Nuggets with a smile. "He was in a coma for ten days."

"Ten days in a coma!" Nuggets said. "That's a long time."

"Sure is," Wally said. "He could hardly open his mouth to talk when he finally regained consciousness."

Remembering that day was easy for J.C. In fact, he remembered everything vividly since then, just nothing that came before. He remembered trying to talk to Wally, the man he shared the hospital room with, but he felt like his mouth was coated with something rough and dry, like fast-drying cement. He remembered Wally calling him Rip Van Winkle, but he didn't know who he was or how he wound up in Sacred Heart Hospital in Greenville, Pennsylvania, or how long he had been there.

That was the first day of his life; he remembered it well. Why wouldn't he? The fugue state didn't damage his brain; it just made him a different person. Otherwise, he seemed to be a healthy young man in his twenties. That was three years ago, the only years stored in his memory bank. Sometimes he feared he would lose those too, the same way he had lost the previous years of his life. He didn't want to start over again.

Three coke-plant workers, covered with eight hours of obfuscate blur, plodded through the entrance and slumped into chairs at a table near the bar. The shortest and dirtiest of the three walked, with mincing steps, to the bar. A cigarette that drooped from his thin, parched lips bobbed with each syllable as he ordered their drinks. J.C. loaded a tray with I.C. Lights that the laborer quickly delivered to his thirsty friends.

"I remember everything that happened the last three years." J.C. said. "Especially when my new life started in that hospital room." He pointed a finger at Wally. "I remember the crush you had on the chubby nurse, Bedpan Betty Moffat."

"I most certainly did not," Wally said waving his hands in a negative motion in front of him.

J.C. squinted at Wally as if he was looking over a pair of glasses. "Come on Wally, she was your squeeze, wasn't she?"

Wally almost jumped off his stool. "Squeeze? I couldn't possibly get my arms around her, let alone squeeze her. She was the size of a refrigerator."

"She squeezed you, I saw her."

"She's a pervert," Wally said, waving his arms again almost knocking his mug over. "She kept trying to fondle my butt."

"You didn't have to fart on her," J.C. said, rolling his eyes. Nuggets stifled a laugh.

"I had to do something," Wally said, "She was molesting me."

Nuggets let out a snicker that turned into a full-fledged, knee-slapping laugh.

Wally's frown slowly turned into a smile. "Give me another beer. Get this young man one too," he said, slapping Nuggets on the shoulder.

J.C. tugged on the Iron City lever and freed its refrigerated amber into tilted glasses, just the way old man Ducheck had taught him. It kept the foam down and the customers happy. It was 7:15, halfway through a Seinfeld rerun. Elaine was just refused cream of broccoli by the Soup Nazi.

The front door swung open. Paul Andrews' 6'2", 230 lb. frame filled the doorway. Clamorous street noise billowed in with him. "How's it goin' guys?"

Paul walked toward the bar, passing the three dirty workmen. They stiffened in their seats. "Good evening, detective," one man said. The other two averted their eyes.

Paul nodded and walked toward the bar. He looked suspiciously at Nuggets before mounting a stool next to Wally.

"What happened in the berg last night?" Wally asked, motioning for J.C. to draw a draft for his nephew.

"Nothing special," Paul said, between puffs on his cigarette, as he tried to light it. "A couple of robberies, three bar fights, two domestics, and some dickhead flasher."

Nuggets noticed Paul looking at the mirrored wall behind J.C. He looked through the whiskey and wine bottles that stood sentinel on the mirror's facade, and saw Paul staring back at him.

"A flasher? No shit?" Wally said with a devilish grin on his face. "Who was the flashee?"

Paul looked away from the mirror toward Wally and grinned, "Three elderly women who belonged to the Saint Edward the Confessor Bridge Club."

They all laughed.

"Did they catch him?" J.C. asked.

"Red-handed, so to speak. Monsignor Rafferty ran the asshole down a couple of blocks from the church. Witnesses said it was quite a sight. A priest running at full speed, his robe flapping, beads and necklaces bouncing and jingling—chasing a man trying to pull his pants up."

J.C.'s smile dissolved into a look of concern. "Anything new on Jason's case?"

Paul drained the remaining beer in his mug. "Nothing new. Forensics is still testing the trash they found in the area; they should be finished soon."

"We found him last Wednesday. It's been six days," J.C. said, his eyes welling up. "Jason's murderer is out there somewhere, enjoying himself, thinking he's safe. He has to be found."

Nuggets leaned forward, a concerned look on his face. "Who's Jason?"

"Jason Saxberg saved J.C.'s life the night he was shot," Wally said. "Jason was driving home at three o'clock in the morning when he saw a flash of light and heard a gunshot near a car parked off the side of the road. As he approached, the car sped off. Jason stopped to investigate and found J.C. near the edge of a rising stream. By stopping, Jason saved J.C. from getting shot again and from drowning."

J.C. noticed Paul staring at Nuggets with a look of distain on his face, a look of *who the hell are you and why are you asking questions?*

"Oh, I'm sorry," J.C. said. "Paul, this is Russell . . . he likes to be called Nuggets."

"Russell what?" Paul asked.

"Russell Payne," Nuggets said, looking suspiciously at Paul. "Why?"

"Just get out of the Army?"

"Yeah. How'd you know?"

"Not too many young men have short hair and wear low quarters," Paul said, looking at Russel's spit-shined shoes. "Just discharged?"

"Yeah, last week. Looking for my aunt. Maybe you can help me? She had a house in the area, Leeds Avenue. Probably couldn't handle the taxes and upkeep; she's probably renting."

"What's her name?" Wally asked.

"Emily. Emily Watkins."

"Is she in the phone book?" J.C. asked.

"No. First place I checked," Nuggets said, holding his head in his hands. "Other than knock on every door in the area, I don't know what to do. She's the only family I have left."

J.C. felt a familiar sense of loss. He knew exactly what it meant not to have a family. For all he knew, he had a family somewhere and they were searching for him.

J.C. looked at Paul with one of those looks that wives use to get their husbands to do their bidding.

"Okay, okay, I'll check it out for you," Paul said, then gestured for another beer. "Where are you staying?"

"At a shelter on Morgan."

At a shelter on Morgan? "He'll be staying here," J.C. said. "There's a spare room upstairs."

Nuggets' jaw fell open. "That's very kind of you but—"

"Nonsense," J.C. said, as he poured Paul's beer. "You'll stay here. You can help out at the bar until you find your aunt."

Paul glared at J.C.

"I know what it's like to have someone reach out a helping hand," J.C. said.

"Today's the anniversary of his death, isn't it?" Paul asked.

J.C. nodded. "July eighth, a year ago today," he said. He felt as if he had lost a father when Charlie Ducheck died. Charlie had taken J.C. in when he didn't have a place to stay and gave him a job. Charlie treated him like a son; he even left him the bar in his will.

Paul and Wally glanced at each other. "I know it's hard," Paul said. "I know how you felt about Charlie. You took his name, out of respect."

Wally looked like he was trying to hold back a grin. "Yeah, from John Doe to John Charlie Ducheck, to J.C."

Seinfeld's Elaine had just pulled a coup d'état on the Soup Nazi. She found his soup recipes and told him, "No soup for you." J.C. cracked a grin. Something Barb, his girl, might do, he thought. She was J.C.'s nurse during most of his stay at the hospital. They had developed a deep relationship. Barb was an only child abandoned by her father when she was three. Her mother died two years later from a rare cancer. Barb had been sent to live with an aunt in Ohio that she hadn't seen before. She sympathized with J.C. and, in a sense, felt his pain.

"What's it been . . . three years?" Paul asked.

"A little over three," J.C. said.

Paul poked Wally in the side. "You had gall bladder surgery then and had the hots for Nurse Betty."

Nuggets grinned, as if he knew where the conversation was going.

"I have a normal sex life; I'm not into bestiality."

"Yeah, you're a regular stud," Paul said.

J.C. wondered about his previous sex life. "I could have been a serial rapist for all I know."

Wally managed a grin, "You could've been a Casanova too."

"Yeah," J.C. said, "I could've been. I could've been a murderer too. How many guys have bullet holes in 'em and can't remember how they got them?"

Wally jumped in. "It could've been a robbery. It could've been a perfectly innocent, tragic thing that happened to you."

"You're forgetting the previous gunshot scar they found," J.C. said. "Word got around pretty fast. Women treated me like a leper. If it wasn't for Barbara I don't know what I'd have done. She's the only woman who took a chance on me, and that's probably because she got to know me in the hospital. I think the world of Barb, but I don't know if I was engaged, married or what. I've got to find out who I am and *what* I am."

"Things'll get better," Wally said. "You'll be able to hire an investigator or do it yourself. You're still going to take that investigator course, aren't you?"

"I'm going to check into it next Monday at the community college. You guys have been an inspiration," J.C. said. "I don't know what I would have done without you." J.C. turned to Nuggets. "Paul checked the surrounding eight counties for me. He even got commander Albright to send my fingerprints to A.F.I.S, the Automated Fingerprint Identification Systems."

"The only advice I have for you," Paul said, "is let the police handle this investigation. Learn to be an investigator if you really want to be one, not because you feel you have to." He hesitated, then continued. "If you have a plumbing problem, you don't run off and learn to be a plumber, do you?"

"This is personal," J.C. said. "If I was an investigator, the first thing I'd do is to find out who murdered Jason."

"Hell yeah," Nuggets said. "He saved your life."

"Yes, he saved my life, but the main reason I'd like to find this low-life is because he's probably the same person who shot me. He knows my name. He knows who I am."

"Really?" Nuggets asked.

"The day before he was murdered, Jason called me with

some interesting information," J.C. said. "He was certain that the man who shot me was also trying to kill him."

Nuggets gulped his beer and leaned forward.

J.C. continued. "Jason had a fire in his apartment two years ago that was ruled suspicious by the fire marshal. Last fall, a bullet narrowly missed him as he drove through Ryerson State Park. The police said it was a hunter's stray bullet."

"Couldn't they be accidents?" Nuggets asked.

"That's what Jason thought," J.C. said. "A week before he called me he was almost run off a cliff by a dark red Buick, the same kind of car he saw fleeing the scene the night I was shot."

"Sounds like the same person," Nuggets said.

J.C. tugged the tap, pouring I.C. Light into a tilted glass. "Maybe not. The guy who killed Jason was in a dark pickup."

"Maybe he stole the truck," Wally said.

Paul finished his beer, shoving the mug to the edge of the bar. "Sounds like a professional. This may take a while."

"That's why I have to find him," J.C. said. "I have more than my life to lose."

"Maybe I'll take that course with you and do some investigating myself," Wally said, slapping his knee. "Hell, since I took my early pension, all I do is take care of my homing pigeons and drink beer. I need something productive to occupy my time."

Paul stood up and walked toward the door. "You can always look up Bedpan Betty."

"I hate to take that crap all the time," Wally said. "If he wasn't my nephew and a cop, I'd have to kick his ass."

Paul turned around. "You two leave this case to the police. We don't need any amateurs going around fucking things up." The lines between his eyes deepened into furrows and he pointed a menacing finger. "Don't let me catch you guys meddling in this case."

Wally scowled at Paul as he left.

A few minutes later, Wally left. J.C. showed Nuggets to his new home and then went to his room and crawled into bed. He thought about what Wally had said. He didn't want to sit around either. He wanted to find Jason's murderer; he wanted to start right away.

Chapter 3

Paul Andrews was a cop, a good cop, one who went by the book, digging out evidence and making note of every detail and rationally piecing it all together for a reliable conclusion.

It was Tuesday, July 9 and Paul had just started the 8x4 shift at the Greenville P.D. Greenville was a medium sized town of about 200,000 nestled at the foot of the Laurel Valley mountain range, about 40 miles southwest of Pittsburgh. Paul, a detective in the Criminal Investigations Division, liked to arrive early, have a cup of coffee with the night shift guys, and get their first-hand account of what happened the night before. It was 08:10 and the desk sergeant was assigning duties to daylight patrolmen when Paul walked through the patrol area with a cup of java. Because Commander Albright hadn't yet arrived, the captain stood watch.

"Call for you Paul," the desk officer said. He handed over the phone to Paul with an outstretched arm, "It's Rixey. He's at the Methodist Church parsonage."

George Rixey was a beat patrolman and Paul's former partner.

Paul took the receiver. "George, what's up?"

"I was just about to go off duty when I heard an ambulance being dispatched to the Smith's, so I decided to check it out." Rixey paused, then said, "I'm sorry Paul, I think the reverend's dead."

"What do you mean, you think?" Paul said, wondering why Rixey didn't get the facts; after all, his parents and the reverend were good friends.

"He didn't appear to be breathing; his daughter was giving him CPR."

"Be right over," Paul said without hesitation. He asked the desk sergeant to tell CID where he was going, that it was a personal thing.

Paul drove Code 3 to the parsonage, a two-story yellow brick house next to the United Methodist Church. He entered through the open front door, surprising Abigail, the reverend's wife, who started to sob when she saw him. She was in the foyer, pacing nervously and crying. She was dressed in black, as usual, with matching shoes and a tiny pillbox hat that sat incongruously on top of her mostly gray hair.

"I'm so very sorry, Mrs. Smith. I just heard. What happened?"

"I don't know . . . he's dead I think," she said between sobs.

"Can I help, ma'am? Where's the reverend?"

Her frail, wrinkled hand clutched a damp hanky. She motioned to the right-angled stairway that led to the second floor.

Rixey stood at the railing on the second-floor balcony. His dark hair and high cheekbones made manifest his Cherokee heritage. He directed Paul to the reverend's bedroom, and went downstairs. The house was a two-story, 1940s vintage, with two rooms on the left side of the hall and one on the right. The reverend's room was at the end of the hallway, on the left.

When Paul entered the bedroom, he saw Ruth, the reverend's daughter, frantically trying to revive her father. She had positioned herself directly over him and was dropping her weight, in a pumping motion, through her straight and rigid arms, onto the reverend's chest, counting: one thousand one; one thousand two; one thousand three until she reached fifteen. She tilted the reverend's head back, checked his airway, then his pulse. Paul didn't know how many times she had repeated this sequence, but guessed it had been a while due to the sweat dripping from her face and the sound of exhaustion in her voice.

Paul knew that the reverend was dead, but didn't want to stop the efforts of a loving daughter.

"Where's that damn ambulance?" Ruth asked between breaths and compressions. "We called fifteen minutes ago."

A nurse at Sacred Heart Hospital, Ruth usually stopped by to see her mother after working the night shift. She was the first born, now in her mid-forties, a slight woman starting to gray. She had changed out of her uniform into a dark blue skirt and matching blouse. Her brother Matthew, who lived across town, was there too, standing at the foot of the bed, sobbing.

The only missing sibling was Mark, Matthew's identical twin. He lived in Fayetteville, North Carolina. The two were complete opposites. Matthew was the quiet, sensitive, clean-cut type. Mark was boisterous and had a reputation as a troublemaker. He dressed flamboyantly, a sign of his rebellion against authority. Mark and the reverend didn't get along at all, unlike Matthew and his father.

"I think that's the ambulance now," Paul said, hearing the faint wail of a siren in the distance. "Open the drapes Matthew, We need some light in here."

Matthew opened the heavy purple drapes and flooded the room with sunlight from the double-hung, sash windows.

The reverend looked peaceful. He lay surrounded by fresh—scented, white linens that brightened up the room's dusky interior. He was dressed in silk burgundy pajamas. Carmine bedding was folded neatly over his lower legs. The sheets were drawn under the reverend's arms, appearing even whiter next to his dark, thick, curly hair. His skin retained a pink hue, but was cold to the touch when Paul took his carotid pulse. The reverend's eyes were shut, his solemn face showed he'd had a merciful, but quick, end the kind that Paul had seen many times before, usually as a result of a heart attack.

When the ambulance arrived, Paul walked to the hallway and watched three paramedics drag their gurney up the wooden stairs, lift it over the railing that was at a ninety-degree angle to the steps, and place it on the landing. They picked up speed, rolling it down the narrow hallway, inadvertently bumping the walls as they went, nearly knocking religious pictures from their moorings. Paul retreated into the bedroom as they converged around the reverend for a preliminary first-aid check. After surveying the scene, the EMT in charge—his nametag read Danoff—checked the reverend's eyes and airway. The family waited for a positive response but got none.

Danoff radioed Sacred Heart Hospital and told the dispatcher that the Reverend was dead. The other two paramedics confirmed the pronouncement with solemn nods. They carefully loaded the reverend's body onto the gurney.

"Where do you want us to take him?" Danoff asked Ruth.

"The Louis Fine Funeral Home?" Ruth said, looking at Matthew for approval. He nodded.

Paul followed them down the stairs. From the foyer, he saw Mrs. Smith sitting in the living room. She jumped up and approached the paramedics with a hopeful, yet knowing expression. Ruth interceded and told her mother that her father was dead. Abigail broke down, sobbing uncontrollably into her handkerchief. Paul offered his condolences and left.

Paul drove the half-mile back to headquarters, trying to justify the passing of such a good man when so many criminals seemed to enjoy good health. His parents had died a few years ago and he remembered the sorrow he felt. He empathized with Ruth and Matthew.

He parked in the space restricted for detectives to the left of the main parking lot, and walked into headquarters. The hexagonal, three-storey lobby provided public access and elevators to all floors.

CID, property division, and the technical support unit were on the second floor and under the command of Captain Leonard Henderson. His office was across from the elevator at the intersection of the two main halls, and could be accessed from either side. Paul usually entered from the CID area. Sharnett, the receptionist and liaison person sat in front of the large-windowed office. The three detectives' desks were in the area to the rear and right. Paul's was at the wall near the window.

He nodded to Sharnett and checked his desk for any new cases and messages. Good news and bad news. The good news was that there weren't any new cases or messages relating to the job. The bad news was that Gerri, his girlfriend, hadn't called confirming their reservation at Rego's, a trendy restaurant on the Upper East Side. Oh well, he needed this time to review the Saxberg case and take his mind off the morning's events.

Paul was reviewing photos of the body and the crime scene, the ME's report, and Saxberg's list of friends and relatives, when Captain Henderson buzzed his intercom.

"Andrews, my office."

"Yes sir," Paul wondered if the captain was going to chew him out for leaving to check on Reverend Smith.

He knocked on the door and entered. The captain looked up from his paperwork. He was a black man of medium build and height. He had a reputation for perseverance. "That's why I got the job," he would say, "not because of quotas."

"I heard about Reverend Smith," he said, studying Paul's face with his large, round eyes. "Come in."

Paul walked to the front of his desk and waited while the captain shuffled some papers.

"Were you close to him?" the captain asked.

"Fairly close, my parents knew him better."

"What did he die from?"

"Looked like a heart attack," Paul said.

"Did you check the reverend's body?"

"No, no reason to . . . why?"

"The reverend was shot, that's why."

Chapter 4

Paul stormed out of headquarters. He jogged to his vehicle and flung the door open, narrowly missing an adjacent car. His sedan lurched forward, leaving black, rubber stains on the asphalt parking lot as he headed for Louis Fine's Mortuary. He violated a red light thinking about the funeral director finding the bullet he had overlooked. He jammed his cigarette butt in the ashtray, sending ashes and sparks flying.

He had made only one other mistake as a police officer. Eight years ago, six months after making detective, Paul and Detective Jessup Kaminski—his partner at the time—entered the third-floor apartment of a suspected drug dealer. It was a mom-and-pop operation—pop being a laid-off steelworker in his thirties trying to make a buck, and mom, a clotheshorse and lover of jewelry.

Paul followed Kaminski's lead, backing him up and checking the rooms while Kaminski apprehended and cuffed the suspects. In the heat of the moment, and focusing on what his partner was doing, Paul hadn't checked the hall closet. When the door burst open and a figure leaped out,

Paul fired his weapon hitting the couple's fourteen-year-old son in the back. The kid's shoulder wound wasn't fatal but it put a blemish on Paul's record and on his memory forever.

That's when the drinking started and the marriage of fourteen years ended. He tried to sort out his problems on his own, but the boozing increased. With help from his uncle Wally and co-workers, he was able to mount a comeback, at least on a functional level. That's when he put aside his regrets and Gerri came into his life. She had been a stabilizing factor in his life but his latest mistake shook him to the core.

But now, Paul had a murder to solve. Captain Henderson had initially assigned all three detectives to the case with Paul as the lead investigator. Two other detectives questioned the family while forensics specialists were sent to preserve what was left of the crime scene. The ME's office was to dispatch a vehicle to pick up the reverend's remains from the mortuary.

Paul had worked on many homicides before and was always quick to find a motive. He knew this case was different; he couldn't believe that anyone would want to shoot Reverend Smith. Paul knew the reverend from the time Paul started to attend church and remembered seeing the reverend greet his parents as they left the Sunday services and how the reverend smiled ever so broadly like politicians do on Election Day. Paul watched him give those "fire and brimstone" sermons and observed how the reverend could be just as gentle holding a baby on its baptism day. Paul saw him as stern to those who needed discipline¾like the kid who tried to set the school on fire. He was also permissive with those who needed guidance, like Paul when he fell asleep at Bible study in Sunday school.

Although Paul respected the reverend, he didn't have any special kind of affection for him and he didn't know why. His parents really admired the reverend and that was good enough for Paul. When Paul's parents passed a few years ago, Reverend Smith genuinely seemed to take it hard.

As Paul walked to the entrance of the funeral home, he had the feeling that Louis Fine would get on his case about missing the reverend's bullet wound. Fine had called the station twice and criticized the slow handling of the Jason Saxberg case; he was persistent and got on Paul's nerves.

Paul heard Fine's voice. "Detective . . . Detective Andrews, over here."

The massive, white colonial two-door entrance framed Fine's lithe, fragile body in a facetious pose. He stood in the doorway smiling; his dark greased head was at an angle. With his left hand on his tuxedo-clad hip and his right arm stretched near the top of the closed door, he spoke through pouting lips covered by a pencil-thin moustache. "I've been waiting for you."

The one-story, red brick building contrasted nicely with its white shutters and accents. Fine exaggerated opening the door as Paul entered the main foyer. Two large chandeliers overhead provided ample light brightening the dark blue wallpaper and heavy mahogany furniture. Light-colored upholstered colonial couches and chairs sat against the main hall walls under ornate, gold-framed mirrors.

Paul knew that four visitation rooms lay off the main hall, two on each side. He entered the first room on the right. Fine was right behind him.

"Well detective . . . do we have an observation problem here?"

Paul didn't want to go there, "Where's the body?"

"Come with me." He gestured, palms-up, as he flung his head back. "Reverend Smith is this way."

Paul followed Louis' duck walk down the Italian marbled hallway to the rear of the building. A glass door, on the left, led to steps that descended to the basement level. The receiving area was in a rear room, behind metal double doors. The reverend lay on a gurney in the middle of the room;

straps from an overhead hoist were still connected under him.

Paul immediately bagged the reverend's hands and carefully looked over the rest of the body. The body's head was turned to the left; its curly hair parted enough to expose what looked like a small caliber bullet wound behind and just beneath the right ear.

Paul looked at Fine. "Did you touch the wound?"

"Of course I did," he said, placing his hands on his hips. "It's part of my job to inspect the body before it gets embalmed." He then looked at Paul and said, "I did *my* job."

Asshole. "I'm trying to do mine now, Louis."

"What about Jason Saxberg? Did you do a good job then?" Fine asked, his voice quivering. "It's been over five days. His body was severely mutilated. It shouldn't be hard to find a pervert who would do something like that."

Paul explained that two crime scene experts found few clues at the scene and that fewer leads had come up since, but the case was open and being investigated in earnest.

"Maybe you didn't look hard enough, just like today?" Louis said, and then started to cry.

"Today's events were very unusual, but don't get upset," Paul said. "We'll find the person responsible for Jason's murder."

Paul told Fine about the unusual circumstances of his visit to the parsonage.

Louis' face contorted in disbelief. "Sounds like murder to me." He looked at the reverend, then at Paul and said, "Could have been suicide, too . . . him being a minister and so forth. You know, the shame of a man of God committing suicide. Maybe the family covered it up."

"Suicide or not, it will be investigated vigorously as a murder, the same as Jason Saxberg's murder."

"You're right Paul. I'm sorry for talking to you like that . . . forgive me?"

I didn't want a hug. "Of course. It's tough losing a good friend."

Now composed, Fine opened the doors to the loading dock at a familiar sound of a horn blast. Paul recognized the letter "B" in Morse code. As the door opened, the ME's driver stood next to his truck.

"I thought he had a heart attack," the driver said with sheepish grin as he walked in.

Paul showed him the wound. The driver shook his head in disbelief, covered the body with plastic and carefully loaded it in the truck.

After the truck left, Paul walked with Fine to the front entrance. Fine apologized for his behavior most of the way. Paul assured Fine the Saxberg case would have the same priority as the reverend's case, although he felt Fine didn't believe him.

Chapter 5

Paul had expected to be called on the carpet before the shift was over. Commander Jack Albright's spacious office was on the third floor next to the chief's and down the hall from the mayor's. Five high-backed upholstered chairs stood at attention in front of the commander's desk. Precinct captains would occupy them at their morning briefings. Paul sat in the center one.

He knew he had screwed up, but not in the same way as in the shooting incident. The commander was leaning forward, over his desk, slowly scanning pages in a manila file. Paul knew it was one of the commander's unnerving techniques; he had experienced it before.

To calm his nerves, Paul studied the details of the room. The wall behind the commander was plastered with pictures of the commander at various ceremonial police and political functions. The top two pictures were, of course, of the mayor and the chief. Two American flags flanked the pictures.

Paul shifted his gaze to the commander's desk. Very neat, he thought, not like the desktops of the officers who did the real work. There was an emerald green in/out tray with a few papers in each compartment. A lime colored leather desk mat covered the mahogany desk, giving it a touch of elegance. A gold plate, bearing the commander's name in old text, separated two bronze statuettes of policemen sat at the edge of the desk. Except for the manila folder, the scene would have made a great picture for *House and Gardens*.

A family photograph in a large, gold frame faced Paul from its position on the left side of the desk. In the photo, the commander was out of uniform; he was wearing a dark blue pin-striped suit. He looked much younger, like a regular person on the street. His wife, Miriam, dressed in an elegant suit, stood next to him. Their sons, Tony and Philip, were seated in front of them.

The picture had to be at least fifteen years old. In it, the boys were teenagers and it had been taken before Philip, the youngest, was institutionalized. Paul remembered that it was due to a nervous breakdown or something similar. Even though he didn't care for the commander, or his methods, he felt a pang of sympathy for him when he looked at the picture. Then he remembered that the commander's brother, Edward, and his wife, tragically were killed four years ago in an auto accident in Oregon. Their only son, John, had joined the Army.

The thought of what the commander must have gone through eased his own feelings about the reprimand he was about to receive.

The commander closed the file he was reading. "What's your gut feeling about the Smith case. Think it's murder?"

Paul was disarmed by the question. "I don't know yet. It could be suicide. Have to wait for the ME's report. Either way, the family's involved."

"I think so too. Check Matthew out thoroughly."

Paul was startled by the commander's instant assessment of the situation. "Sure. Do you have any information on Matthew?"

"No. Just a hunch. Check him out." The commander opened another file on his desk. "That's all."

Paul left, wondering why he didn't get chewed out and whether the commander had information about Matthew that he couldn't or didn't want to share.

#

That evening, at Ducheck's bar, Paul voiced his indignation over the day's events.

"Never saw anything like it in my twenty-four years on the force," Paul said, nervously combing his fingers through his thick, mousy-brown hair. "Made me look like a fuckin' rookie, not a detective."

Not only was Paul upset about missing the gunshot wound, but also because Gerri had gone on a buying trip for the Brunei Art Museum. She had worked for the museum for twelve years, working her way up through the ranks to buyer.

Paul had met Gerri Terensky five years after his wife left him. Gerri's companionship erased most of the guilt and sleepless nights he had over the shooting incident. She was his strength and he needed to be with her, especially after today's events. But now their dinner plans were cancelled.

"Who would expect something like that?" J.C. said, pouring another draft for Wally and a double bourbon for Paul. "It's not your fault. Looks like a cover-up."

Wally nodded in agreement only after staring sarcastically at the whiskey Paul had ordered. They had been alone at the bar when Paul described the scene at the parsonage, but when a bowling team showed up, J.C. suggested they move to the back room. He knew Paul didn't like discussing police business in public.

J.C. picked up the phone and punched in Nuggets' number. He heard the phone ring once just as Nuggets came around the corner from the back room.

J.C. cradled the phone when he saw him. "Can you take care of some thirsty bowlers? It'll only be a few minutes."

"Hell yes. Take all the time you need. Looks like I came just in time."

J.C. felt good that he was helping Nuggets as Charlie had helped him. Nuggets would have a place to stay, while searching for his aunt, and earn some spending money too.

They carried their drinks into the back room. Paul and Wally slid into their usual booth at the far corner of the room. J.C. sat on the aisle. It was the largest booth and could accommodate six people. On good nights, the jukebox would be playing and people would be cheering on their favorite sports team, but like most weekdays, the room was empty.

"You mentioned a cover-up," Paul said, shifting his gaze from his frosted mug to J.C. "You're thinking it's a murder cover-up, right?"

"Well . . . yeah."

"It could be a cover-up for suicide," Paul said. "Maybe the wife, the son, or the whole family for that matter, decided that suicide wasn't a proper way for the reverend to be remembered. Maybe they cleaned up the reverend and his room hoping the wound wouldn't be discovered."

"Bizarre, totally bizarre," Wally said, "but I can understand Abigail not wanting the reverend's death to be a suicide."

Nuggets appeared at their table. "Need anything?" he said. Nobody answered. "I'll be by the window. Just holler." He pointed to a small serving window on the wall that separated the back room from the bar as he walked away.

"The ME will determine the cause of death," Paul said, watching Nuggets walk toward the bar. "If he was murdered, it could be a tough case to solve, and I don't need another tough one." Paul then started talking about the Saxberg case. He explained that forensics had come up with little evidence because of the heavy rain that night and because the crowd contaminated the scene.

The way Paul was talking, J.C. sensed that the reverend's case was going to get most of the attention and Jason's less. As he listened to Paul's briefing on the Saxberg murder,

J.C. felt a connection to Jason Saxberg that he hadn't experienced before. Hearing Paul talk about the grisly details of Jason's murder, the similarity of their lives became more evident to him. They were both ostracized by the community—Jason because he was homosexual, J.C. because of his suspicious and uncertain past. He felt Jason's pain. He wanted to find Jason's murderer, not only out of obligation to Jason, but for himself as well. Jason's murderer was probably the only person who knew his identity. To find this man J.C. knew he needed help, someone to kick around his ideas with. He needed a partner.

"Maybe we can talk over the Saxberg case sometime," Wally said looking at J.C. as if he had read his mind. "Maybe we can do a little investigating on the side, you know . . . as private citizens."

"That would be great," J.C. said.

Paul slammed his mug on the table, splashing beer and foam onto the table. "I told you before to stay out of it. Leave it to the professionals. Civilians only get in the way."

Wally and J.C. looked at each other with eyebrows raised as if they knew they were going to defy Paul's order.

Paul stormed out of the room and headed into the bar area.

Wally watched him disappear around the corner. "The Smith case has Paul back on the hard stuff. Now he's upset about the Saxberg case. He told me that a lawyer prevented him from questioning two young men."

J.C. leaned forward. "Did he say who they were?"

"No, just that one of the young men's father is a lawyer and put a stop to any questioning."

"Maybe we can find out who these guys are."

"We'll have to do it on our own," Wally said. "Paul won't tell me anything."

"That's where we'll start then."

Chapter 6

Wally woke up earlier than usual, excited about the new partnership with J.C. Solving Jason's murder was secondary to him; discovering J.C.'s identity was his main concern. After eating breakfast and feeding his pigeons, Wally drove to Ducheck's. The bar was strategically located on the corner of Second and Linden, across from the millgate entrance to the blast furnaces. Wally parked his Chevy pickup in front of the bar. He remembered when business was good and parking spaces were scarce—a block's walk wasn't unheard of—two on payday. That was about fifteen years ago when Charlie ran the bar and the mills were working three shifts. A crowd would normally come in after the 4X12 and 12X8 shifts; daylight workers would usually patronize the place during the evening.

The facade of the building reflected a fifties attempt to up-scale retro thirties. Fieldstone covered the first floor and brown aluminum siding, pitted by acids and dust from the mill, hung from the second. The corner entrance provided easy accessibility from both streets through a tall, forty-inch wide door.

The suction created when Wally opened the door hit him with a blast of stale hops, whiskey, and cheap cigar and cigarette smoke. His eyes started to water.

The balls on the pool table sat still as did the tipless cue sticks that stood sentinel against the near wall. The place was empty, except for Jack "Quack" Lenhardt who perched on one of the red-upholstered, chrome-legged bar stools talking to J.C. Jack drank every day—whiskey shots chased by beer. He usually started after lunch and spouted his opinions about economics until dinner. After dinner, politics was the favorite subject.

J.C. stood in front of the smoke and age-stained mirror that was the bar's backdrop for the glass shelves supporting liquor bottles of various shapes and colors. Vertical neon lights at the ends of the bar accentuated the bottles like so many brightly colored jewels. J.C. leaned on the dark-stained oak bar with both palms down, as if they were nailed there. He raised them slowly with a look of relief when he saw Wally.

"Nuggets," Jack almost fell off his stool by J.C.'s voice. "Can you take over?"

"Sure thing," a voice echoed from the back room.

Nuggets came in and assumed his working position, elbows on the bar and a concerned look on his face. He took over listening to Jack's opinions about the world's economy and the cartel that controlled it.

J.C. and Wally walked toward the back room. J.C. flicked sawdust on the shuffleboard, as if shooing a bug and noticed a flickering light bulb above one of the tables that needed to be replaced.

"When do you want to get started?" J.C. asked eagerly, sliding into the booth making a farting sound as he slid across the worn leather.

"As soon as you wipe your ass," Wally said with a grin.

J.C. looked embarrassed. He opened his mouth to explain but stopped when he saw the grin on Wally's face. "I've been thinking about it," he said. "We should talk to

Saxberg's mother first and find out what the police wanted to know. Maybe we can get her to remember something she didn't tell them."

Nuggets appeared at the serving window, his elbows resting on the sill, his hands clasped together as if in prayer. "You guys want anything?"

"No thanks," they both said in unison.

"Yeah, that's a good idea," Wally said. "And we should get a copy of the funeral home visitation list from her; it might prove useful. Maybe we can get the names of the boys Paul talked to."

"Asking about his friends would be a start," J.C. said. "Then we need to find a motive. By the way, the boys will talk to us won't they?"

"I'll tell them I'm Paul's uncle and, if they ask, you're a private investigator."

"Who would I say I'm representing?"

"If you're a private investigator, it's private, isn't it?"

J.C.'s eyebrows registered the logic. "Sounds like a plan."

J.C. told Nuggets he'd be back in a few hours. They left the bar, jumped in Wally's pickup, and headed for the Saxberg residence, across town to Dutchtown. The house was a white colonial accented in black. It sat on a large lot with plenty of shrubbery.

Wally introduced himself and J.C. to Mrs. Saxberg, a portly woman in her fifties and explained the reason for their visit. She had silver hair and flawless alabaster skin accented by pouty red lips and ice-blue eyes. She was about 5' 2" and looked up to Wally as she listened to him. After Wally lied and said that his grandson was very good friends with Jason, she agreed to talk to them. They entered the living room and sat on an overstuffed blue velvet couch.

"Would you like a cup of tea?" she asked.

"No thank you, ma'am," Wally said.

"Call me Gloria," she said with a wink and sat on a divan next to the coffee table. "What can I do to help you boys?"

"Do you have the visitation list from the funeral home?" J.C. asked.

"Why yes, I just finished the thank-you notes."

"Could we have a copy of it ma'am, I mean Gloria," J.C. asked.

"Why certainly; it's no bother. I made one for the police a couple of days ago." She got up and went into a rear room.

"So far so good," Wally said.

J.C. stood up and walked to the fireplace, noticing framed photographs on the mantel.

J.C. heard Mrs. Saxberg's footsteps and turned away from the fireplace, not noticing anything particularly helpful.

"Here you are, boys," she said, waving the list. She handed it to J.C.

"That was quick," J.C. said.

"I have a copier. I'm an interior decorator," she said. "Do you need my services?"

"Uh, not at the moment," J.C. said, blushing.

"Anything else I can do for you?"

Wally asked about Jason's closest friends. J.C. made notes on the list as Mrs. Saxberg named them.

"Do you know of anyone who might have a motive to kill your son?" J.C. asked.

Her expression changed from concern to one of disbelief. "No, no I don't know who would want to hurt my Jason. He was such a good boy."

"What about these boys?" J.C. asked, referring to the funeral home list. "Were any of them different from the rest of his friends?"

"What do you mean different? They're all different."

"I mean being different from your average twenty-four year-old," J.C. said, "like someone who's too religious or too—"

"I really didn't know his friends that well, but I heard one policeman talking to another about Herman Nicklaus and Jimmy Restivo."

J.C. and Wally looked at each other as if they had just been presented with a gift, the names they were looking for.

"Jimmy Restivo?" Wally asked.

"Yes, Jimmy Restivo," Mrs. Saxberg said. "He's a very religious boy, but he wasn't a real close friend to Jason. I have a picture of him; would you like to see it?"

"Yes, I would," J.C. said. He got up and walked across the room to the mantel where Mrs. Saxberg had picked up a picture. Wally followed.

"This is a picture of the high school choir. Jason was in it," she said. "This is Jimmy Restivo." She pointed to a curly-haired, thin boy with an angelic face.

"What about Herman Nicklaus?" J.C. asked. "What did the police say about him?" All three paced back toward the couch.

"The one policeman said he was a real right-winger," she said. "What does that mean?"

"We'll try to find out," Wally said. "Are there any others the police talked about?"

She scanned the list. "I don't think so."

"That's all for now Mrs. Saxberg. If you think of anything else, call this number." Wally handed her one of J.C.'s computer-generated business cards.

They got in Wally's pickup and headed for Ducheck's Bar.

Four patrons were arguing politics, so Wally and J.C. headed to the back room and their favorite booth.

"Do you think Restivo and Nicklaus are the two names that were given to Paul?" J.C. asked.

"Could be. But it could be anyone. Paul said that no one was talking, that they didn't want to be associated with a murder of a homosexual."

"Maybe we can find information that the police can't."

"How's that?"

"We have two names," J.C. said, "Two young men the

47

police were interested in and the questioning was stopped by a lawyer. All we have to do is watch them and look for an opportunity."

"You mean like a surveillance?" Wally asked.

"Exactly."

"All right. Let's meet tomorrow," Wally hesitated. "But first, let me check on the names Restivo and Nicklaus in the Yellow Pages. If we have a match, it's a go. Okay?"

"Good thinking, Wally. Check it out. What's going on later?"

"I'm going to meet Paul this afternoon at the funeral home."

"Sounds like fun. Is Paul there on business or paying his respect?"

"A little of both," Wally said.

Chapter 7

Paul would rather go over a ballistics report than have coffee with the night shift guys. He didn't want to hear the load of crap they'd give him over the Smith debacle, such as: "The heart attack was bad, but the bullet in the head was a real killer;" "Maybe you should partner up with Louis Fine. At least he would know a homicide when he saw one;" or, "Maybe it was the immaculate deception." Worse yet, maybe some of the younger, macho beat cops, who had a grudge against authority, might make a crack about his earlier shooting of a teenager.

The crime scene unit brewed their special blend in chemistry beakers, but it was better than no coffee at all. Mike, the junior member of the team, had already made the coffee.

"Got anything on the Smith case?"

"Not much, the scene wasn't preserved." He shot a quick glance at Paul, and then recovered by saying, "The family did a good job of cleaning up."

"Right," Paul said as he bent over to look into a microscope thinking about the concern the commander had about Matthew. "A lot of people were in that room, tramping around and touching things."

"Dan got the bullet and gunshot residue from the ME a couple of minutes ago," Mike said as they walked past the chemical and blood analysis equipment. "That might help."

"It might if we had a firearm to match it to," Paul said, checking his enthusiasm. "Thanks anyway. I'll be back after I go over the ME's report."

Paul walked down the corridor to C.I.D. and sat at his desk. The other detectives were already working when Paul entered. Captain Henderson walked up and nonchalantly dropped a folder on Paul's desk and walked away. It was the ME's report on Reverend Smith. Paul normally wouldn't mind having two cases at the same time—he had more sometimes—but having two that were leading nowhere was a bit overwhelming.

After Paul read the ME's report, he gave it to Sharnett and asked her to make two copies. She left for the copy room down the hall. Paul figured Pastor and Phillips would offer some assistance; they didn't have a heavy workload. Pastor was working on the kidnapping of a three-year old, probably carried out by the mother's estranged husband, and a drive-by retaliatory gang shooting. Phillips had a home invasion-rape case and a theft of eighty pounds of Chocolate Bunny ice cream from a Dairy Queen on Fifth Street. When Sharnett returned, she gave the copies to Paul, which he distributed to the other detectives.

Although very professional in his scientific method and diagnosis, Doctor DeVane was crude when performing his job. Paul would rather read his report than watch him work. The autopsy report began in a logical manner with the cause of death, in this case a gunshot wound. The report included photographs of the body and wounds followed by an X-ray that revealed a metallic object in the occipital lobe of the brain. An examination of the entrance wound found that it was in the right temporal bone, 6.25 centimeters to the rear of the external auditory meatus. In layman's terms, he was shot behind the right ear and the bullet was lodged at the top rear of the reverend's head.

The ME's report stated that, after the paper bags were removed from the victim's hands, adhesive tape was applied to them in order to collect any gunshot residue. The report described the wound and how the ME recovered residue from inside the entrance wound, but found none around the wound.

The X-ray determined the bullet's location and facilitated its removal. The ME also found a one-and-a-half centimeter hematoma on the left side of the reverend's head, midway between his ear and eye. DeVane had obtained toxicology evidence and sent it to the lab with the bullet and residue samples. The report concluded with the ME's finding: death by homicide.

Paul finished reading the report and called the ME.

"Dr. DeVane, Paul Andrews, I have some questions on the Smith autopsy report."

"Okay, let me get my notes," Paul heard the sound of the phone dropping onto something hard, then papers being shuffled in the distance. A short time later, he heard footsteps getting louder. Then the phone was picked up.

"What can I help you with?" Doctor Devane said.

"My first question is about the lack of gunshot residue around the wound."

"Good question. That's because it was a hard contact gunshot wound."

Paul waited for an explanation.

"The barrel of the gun was pressed hard against the head forcing all gunshot residue into the wound. That's where I found it."

"That makes sense. I noticed on your report the entrance angle of the wound is in a position that might indicate he couldn't have shot himself. Is that true?"

"The location and angle of the wound are not consistent

with a suicide. However, if you notice that the angle I have listed is approximate. It's possible. He could have turned his head and used a short-barreled weapon."

"What about blood? Would there have been a lot of it from this wound?"

"No, very little if any. He died instantly, stopping the flow of blood."

"What about a vein or artery at the wound?" Paul asked. "Wouldn't it cause a loss of blood?"

"Normally it would cause some loss, but in this case the bullet missed the posterior auricular artery."

"One more question, doc," Paul said, hoping for an answer that would give him a direction to follow. "What can you tell me about the hematoma on the reverend's head? What do you think caused it? Could it have been from hitting the nightstand?

"It was fresh and the depression on the reverend's head was inconsistent with anything in the area," Doctor Devane said. "In my opinion, the hematoma could have resulted from being hit by an object similar to the handle of a pistol. That, plus the entrance angle of the bullet led me to the conclusion that a murder had indeed occurred."

Paul thanked the coroner and hung up the phone wondering if the commander actually had some information about the reverend's death. Why did he want Matthew investigated? Why was he so sure it was murder? To find out, he had to investigate, and the first place to go was the forensic lab. Before he left, he made a copy of the ME's report, highlighting the parts of it that were of interest. It was easier than taking notes.

Sergeant Franklin was in the ballistics area of the lab sitting on a stool at a large worktable.

"Here's the bullet," he said, taking the small irregular shaped piece of lead from the scale. "Forty five grams, looks like a twenty-five auto. It's pretty deformed."

That goes along with DeVane's theory, Paul thought. A short-barreled gun was used, which would describe a twenty-five automatic.

"It ricocheted around the inside of the reverend's skull," Franklin said.

"Chopped up his brain pretty good?"

"Yeah, that's because its muzzle velocity is relatively slow, eight hundred and fifteen feet per second. A twenty-five is less potent than a twenty-two; it didn't penetrate the other side of the skull."

"What about residue?" Paul asked, hoping for something substantial.

"The wound sample had gunpowder and lead residue leading me to believe that it was older ammo. Do you have the weapon?"

"No," Paul said. "What about the taped hand samples."

"Nothing."

"What did your guys find at the scene?"

"Tomaskovic checked for latents while Bianchi did the paperwork. They bagged the prescription bottles on the nightstand. The bed, bedding, drapes, and floor were vacuumed separately."

"What about luminol?" Paul asked.

"Absolutely, But no blood was found. Sorry I can't help you more. Finding the weapon would help a lot."

"I guess the toxicology report will take a while?"

"It'll be around five weeks."

"Thanks, I appreciate it."

Since there was little evidence, Paul hoped that going to the reverend's wake would provide more insight into the murder.

Chapter 8

Paul arrived at Louis Fine's Funeral home at 3:30, thirty minutes before the scheduled visitation. The parking lot was barren. As he opened the right door of the massive set of colonials, the strong scent of artificial spring assailed his sinuses. A black sign above the far right door displayed the name: REVEREND JAMES SMITH. The other empty rooms would provide waiting areas for the large number of visitors that were sure to come.

Overhead lighting illuminated the rainbow of colors painted on the marcelled arrangements and bouquets of flowers surrounding the lifeless body of the reverend. Paul walked over to the casket to pay his respects. The reverend's head rested on a lavender plush pillow that hid any evidence of his wound. Paul touched the casket. Its metallic shell was cold and smooth.

Soft music began to emanate from overhead speakers, signaling that the body was now available for viewing.

Paul went across the hall to a vacant room. He wanted to observe the family's reactions without being seen. He sat in a high-backed wing-tipped chair, sucking on hard candy that Louis Fine provided for mourners, and waited.

The family arrived at 3:50, Abigail leading the way. She looked the same in mourning as she did in everyday life. She wore black clothing and shoes, and a black pillbox hat as she always seemed to—this time the hat supported a veil. Ruth, Matthew, and Mark trailed behind Abigail like dutiful chicks following their mother hen. Mark's long hair was draped over his blue print sport shirt. Matthew's black suit matched Ruth's plain black dress.

When a family first views a departed loved one, it's usually a very emotional situation. Not in this case. There was no wailing, no crying, nor any sign of emotion from the reverend's family. Were their religious beliefs that strong? Paul had witnessed people with strong religious convictions who didn't show any emotion. They almost always had a sense of peace and serenity on their faces—the Smith family didn't.

The first group of people to arrive was the older members of the church; those who were too frail to visit their families or shop for a birthday gift, but always had the time to make it to funerals. The receiving line was set up in reverse of the way the family had entered, chicks in a row ending with the mother hen.

Paul watched an old friend of Mrs. Smith's bottleneck the line by reliving decades of old memories with Abigail, who tolerated chatting with her. There's at least one *bottlenecker* in every funeral reception line followed by squirming, weight-shifting, impatient people, all wanting to pay their respects and get the hell out of there.

Women hugged the Smiths while expressing their sorrow; men shook their hands. Businessmen and politicians hugged and shook hands. A retired physics teacher did neither; she confirmed her existence by visiting the dead.

A stocky man in a plaid flannel shirt bucked the line by pulling an end-around. Paul recognized him as the man who ran the church's *"Las Vegas Nights"* that the reverend frequently sponsored to raise money for the church. The man went straight to the casket to pay his respects and then back-peddled into the receiving line. There's at least one end-around at every visitation.

Commander Jack Albright appeared at the entrance of the room with his younger son Tony and his wife Miriam. They were dressed to the hilt. Thanks to an inheritance from his uncle Bertram, the commander could afford such luxuries. Tony had the yellowish-green remains around his eyes from what could only be from black eyes. The commander explained to Paul that Tony was mugged a few weeks ago and joked that he had to write the report himself since Tony had reported the incident to him at home.

Paul spotted his Uncle Wally in the reception line talking to the widow Beechford. It looked as if he had raided the wardrobe department of a gangster movie. He was wearing a 1920s zoot suit, complete with watch pocket chain and black-and-white oxfords. He casually held a fedora with his left hand. Paul thought Wally had dressed like a wise guy because he was under the assumption that the reverend was murdered. Paul hadn't told Wally about the ME's report yet. The widow Beechford seemed to like Wally's outfit— she was about the same age. She left when Paul motioned for Wally.

"Nice outfit," Paul said, looking over Wally's bizarre outfit. "Looking to rub somebody out?"

"No, just rub somebody," Wally said, "and you chased her away."

"I just called you over. I didn't chase her away . . . Who's that?" Paul said, motioning toward a man talking to Abigail.

"That's the Bishop of the Pittsburgh Episcopal area," Wally said. "Looks like he's creating a bottleneck."

Paul wanted to get close enough to hear what the bishop was saying but noticed Mark was walking away, toward the front room. "Wally, see what Mark's up to," Paul said. Without waiting, Paul edged forward to try and hear some of the conversation between Abigail and the bishop while keeping an eye on Matthew. By the time Paul maneuvered his way through the crowd, however, the bishop was walking away.

Wally came back a few seconds later, his shoulders hunched and his eyebrows raised.

"What's the matter?" Paul asked.

"She left."

"Who left?"

"The girl Mark was talking to."

"Why'd she leave?"

"I don't know, she just left" Wally said, "I didn't hear what they said, but Mark was motioning for her to leave."

"What'd she look like?"

"Just a kid. Pretty with red hair."

"How old?"

"Probably in her twenties," Wally thought forty was young. "Are you coming back this evening?"

"Yeah, after I take a nap and shower. Then I have to check out an alibi this evening—at a gay bar."

"Really, can I tag along?" Wally asked. "What case is it?"

"Saxberg. I'd rather go alone."

"Wouldn't it look better if J.C. and I went with you, you know for the look of it?"

Paul thought it might be best to let them tag along. Since he was off duty they'd only follow him anyway.

"I'll pick you up at home, after the wake, about ten o'clock."

When Wally arrived home, he called J.C. and told him about Paul's off-duty interview.

#

J.C. was anxious. He left the bar at nine-thirty and pottered around in his apartment for half an hour before leaving. He slid his six-one frame into Charlie's old Bronco and heading for Wally's. Since Barb was working the 4X12 shift, J.C. thought it would be a good opportunity for him to watch Paul's technique. He wanted to study the case and ultimately, in his mind, see himself solving it. He had been in a fog for the past three years, waiting for the police to discover what others couldn't—his identity. Finding Jason's murderer was the key. J.C. arrived at Wally's fifteen minutes early. Paul was already seated on Wally's couch, watching TV.

Wally was dressed in a chartreuse, puffy shirt, baggy dark green slacks and patent leather shoes. His gray hair was slicked down with some kind of greasy substance and he had a clip-on earring attached to his left ear.

J.C. thought Wally looked like an effeminate buccaneer. "Where's your miniature poodle?" Wally was silent. Paul stifled a grin as he punched the TV remote, turning off a re-run of "*Dragnet*".

They got into Paul's Blazer and headed north toward The Velvet Slipper.

"Are we there yet?" Wally asked.

"About six blocks," Paul said.

"Sounds like you've been in this place before," Wally said grinning. He elbowed J.C. Wally welcomed paybacks.

The smiling doorman greeted the trio as they entered the sweet-smelling interior of the one-storey building. A lobby and coatroom led to an area of tables that surrounded a dance floor. A suspended, rotating three-foot mirrored globe produced muted patches of pastel colors that danced over close-held couples on the floor. An elliptical bar separated the dance area from a smaller, elevated platform where shadowy figures paused at the trio's entrance.

Round, rose-colored ceiling lights shown down on the bar. Two young, dark-haired bartenders were on duty, both wearing "puffy" shirts like Wally's, only white.

"IC Light and a double Bellows," Paul said to the nearest bartender. J.C. ordered a Stoney's.

The bartender efficiently de-capped the brew and placed the bottle in front of J.C. and then poured a double for Paul.

"What'll you have, sir?" the other bartender asked, looking at Wally.

"I'd like a blowjob," Wally blurted at about ninety decibels.

It seemed as if time had stopped. Paul looked pissed, J.C. snorted beer through his nose.

An old drunk at the end of the bar said, "Ill have the same."

Paul shook his head. He could never predict what Wally would do when identifying with his environment. Paul flashed his tin at the bartender who had waited on him. "I'd like to ask you a few questions."

"I really can't, I'm on duty," he said, canting his head with a cocky attitude.

"I can ask you a couple of questions here or I can ask them downtown. It really doesn't make a difference to me."

"Okay, okay what do you want?" The bartender said, spreading his palms on the bar.

J.C. was impressed. He saw how authority could motivate a person to a quick response. He wished it could be this easy to find Jason's murderer, but knew it would be a lot harder. After all, Paul and Commander Albright had tried for years to find his identity—and Albright was a police commander. It would be a lot harder for a novice to solve a murder.

"I want to know about Lawrence Bovine," Paul said. "Was he here on the night of June fourth, and at what time?"

"What day was that?"

"Tuesday. You know what day I'm talking about, the day Jason Saxberg was murdered."

"Yeah he was here."

"What time did he leave?" Paul asked, looking at the bartender's face for a sign of deceit.

J.C. studied the urgency in Paul's face as he questioned

the bartender, then observed the man's responses, looking for any sign that he was lying.

"Eleven thirty," he said with a straight face.

"How can you be sure?" Paul asked.

"Because the news was just over and he said something about the Pirates as he left," he said.

"That's right," a young woman said stepping out of the crowd. Conversation stopped and heads turned. She was a light-skinned black woman with short hair that framed a face that had big, brown eyes and full lips. "I saw him leave that night, and it was eleven thirty."

"What's your name?"

"Leslie Carter. Anything else?"

"No, I don't think so," Paul said, staring at her beauty. "Here's my card. Give me a call if you hear anything, will you?" He fumbled for a card in his wallet.

J.C. thought Paul looked infatuated unlike the woman and was surprised that a police detective didn't recognize a transvestite. He looked at Wally and smiled. Wally raised his eyebrows.

As they left, Paul was smiling.

Paul started up the Blazer and ran over part of the curb as he left the parking lot.

"Nervous?" Wally asked.

"No, why?"

"I thought you might be nervous, that's all."

"All right," Paul said, "what's this all about?"

"Nothing," he said with a slight grin on his face. "I just thought you were nervous with that transvestite coming on to you, that's all."

Paul drove home in silence.

Chapter 9

The opposite of boredom is anxiety and J.C. had it in spades. His desire to find Jason Saxberg's murderer, and ultimately his own identity, suddenly became an obsession. He needed help with surveillance and Wally fit the bill, but he was late as usual. J.C. checked his watch for the tenth time and was wiping a clean bar out of compulsion.

Random streaks of morning light burst through the holes in the tattered blind over the east window, crossing over the aging neon Budweiser sign and exaggerating the grain in the floor. The light played off the unwashed, oily face of an alcoholic who was sleeping at the bar.

Wally leaped through the door, fashionably late. He looked like a bad imitation of a famous fictional detective. He wore a flowing gray plaid cape and deerstalker hat.

The alcoholic's head rose in a jerking motion as if attached to a child's Tinker Toy crane. He looked around with bleary eyes that seemed to be watching an imaginary tennis game.

"Where's your pipe and magnifying glass, Sherlock?" J.C. asked.

"Stifle it, Watson," Wally joked back.

The narcoleptic's noggin hit the bar with a thud.

Wally slid onto the red, padded barstool. The expression on his face looked like a child's when opening a Christmas present. "I checked the yellow pages under lawyers. There's a Restivo listed. It's got to be the same Restivo who halted the investigation of his son, the kid the cops wanted to talk to. When do we get started? Do we work separately? At the same time? What do we need? Surveil—is that a word?"

"Whoa, slow down," J.C. said, reaching for a pad and pencil under the bar. "Let's take this one at a time. We should work together. We're a team, right?" Wally smiled. J.C. started writing. "Besides, who would suspect the two of us on a surveillance?"

"Right," Wally said, "three of a kind can't beat this pair. What do we need? How about binoculars?"

"I thought about that. From what I learned at the camera shop at the mall, a video camcorder is what we need. They magnify much more than a thirty-five millimeter and you can videotape as well. Do you have one?"

"Paul does. I'll use his. What else?"

"Wear dark clothes in case we have to walk around at night. Bring a dress jacket in case we have to go into a restaurant or club."

"I see you've been thinking about this. Sounds logical so far. What else?"

"We'll need a cooler with drinks," J.C. said as he pointed toward a medium-sized cooler on the floor, "and snacks."

"I'll whip up some snacks. Anything else?"

"One more thing. Do you have a dog leash and collar?"

"Yeah . . . what the hell for?

"Lighten up. I wasn't going to ask you to wear it. It's a cover in case a noisy neighbor or someone gets suspicious. We'll say we're looking for your lost dog."

"That's great. How did you think that one up?"

"I got the idea on the Internet. I downloaded a picture of a Doberman Pinscher, and made a few copies; in case anyone asks."

"Looks like we have everything we need," Wally said.

"We'll have to use your truck. Charlie's old Bronco is in the garage. It needs brakes and exhaust work for inspection."

"No problem," Wally said. "Who's the first lucky surveilee?"

"I thought Herman Nicklaus would be a logical first choice. I heard skinheads don't like gays."

Wally didn't argue. "I have black clothes, but nothing in leather."

"Pick me up at seven o'clock. I'll have Nuggets tend bar."

Wally adjusted his deerstalker hat as he got up to leave. "Seven o'clock it is then," he said, and left.

#

Wally arrived at the bar on time and was sipping a beer. He was dressed all in black like a cat burglar. A black ski mask was hanging out of his rear pocket.

"What about face paint?" J.C. asked. "Sylvester Stallone would use it."

"It's in my pocket. I didn't want to give away our operation."

Nuggets walked around the corner just as J.C. was about to pick up the phone.

"Just in time," J.C. said. "I was about to call you. Can you take care of the bar?"

"Absolutely," Nuggets said, walking behind the bar.

"If we're late, lock up."

Nuggets wheeled around. "Do you think the surveillance will last that long?"

Wally drained the remainder of his beer. "Don't know how long it will take."

J.C. shrugged his shoulders, picked up the cooler he had prepared and followed Wally to his truck. Wally's plastic picnic basket was in the middle of the front seat. J.C. put his cooler on the floor, under the dash.

Wally started the old Chevy and coaxed the manual shift into gear. They drove to the northwest part of the city and found the house at the end of a quarter-mile road on a culdesac, #765. It was a large English Tudor, like many of the other houses in the wealthy neighborhood. Mercedes, BMWs and Toyota Land cruisers were prominent, mostly silver in color.

"Where will we surveil from?" Wally asked. "Their lawns go right to the road. Don't these people know about sidewalks?"

"The people that live in these houses don't walk, they ride. What about here?" J.C. pointed to a grassy area in front of an electrical utility transformer. The fence that surrounded it had a sign on it that read: DANGER HIGH VOLTAGE.

"Did you bring any hard hats?" Wally asked.

"No, they wouldn't do us any good anyway. We don't have a utility vehicle. And besides, these people won't care as long as we're not on their lawns."

"What does Nicklaus drive?" Wally asked.

"I don't know."

"I thought it'd be parked outside."

"Did you notice a car outside?"

"No."

"Here," J.C. said, "take this dog leash and poster. Walk past the house. See if you can spot a vehicle in the garage."

"Why can't we drive past and look?"

"It would arouse suspicion. We've already driven past once. If we drive past again, we'll be made."

"Okay," Wally said, reaching for his can of face paint.

"You won't need that looking for a dog, will you?"

Wally agreed. He grabbed the leash and poster and got out of the truck. "Be back in a minute."

Five minutes later, Wally returned, dragging the leash on the ground. "It's a red, Dodge Ram pickup with a

Confederate flag in the back window. I didn't get the plate number.

"Good work. "Now we know what to look for."

"Now it's time to eat," Wally pressed a button on the side of the picnic basket and swiveled the top to the side. "It's seven thirty."

Wally devoured two hard-boiled eggs before J.C. could determine what was in the basket.

"Is that it?" J.C. asked. "Pepperoni sticks, cheese and eggs?"

"There's two peanut butter sandwiches," Wally said. "What drinks did you bring?"

"Pepsi and ginger ale."

The light of day finally disappeared as did the hard-boiled eggs, cheese and pepperoni sticks. Four empty soda cans littered the floor. It was approaching ten o'clock and a variety of residents vehicles had driven by, some people looking cautiously at them—most didn't bat an eyelash.

"I've got to pee," J.C. said. *Mistake number one.* "We can't leave. Where can I go?"

"There's some bushes on the other side of that transformer. Go there," Wally said. "But be careful not to spray the metal fence or you'll light up like a Christmas tree."

J.C. managed to relieve himself without being electrocuted or seen by nearby neighbors. As he walked back to the truck, he heard the sound of an approaching vehicle. He dove in through the passenger side door and checked his side mirror.

"Here comes the Dodge," J.C. said. "Start the truck."

Wally had the keys in his pocket. *Mistake number two.* He straightened his right leg to reach in his pocket for the keys and his foot hit the accelerator, flooding the carburetor. He jammed the ignition key home and turned it, only to hear the mechanical equivalent of rap music. The engine churned and churned with each attempt. "Son of a bitch," he said.

He held the pedal to the floor as he turned the key again.
The truck finally started and they sped off, the wheels
spinning on the loose gravel and pinging small stones off
the chain link fence that surrounded the transformer.

"Hurry up Wally, he's getting away," J.C. strained his eyes
looking for taillights through the trees and brush. "There
he is. Turn left. He's on Beechwood. He's headed for town."

Wally followed the red Dodge for about a mile, until it
turned right on Route #136 West.

"You didn't have to go through those three red lights,
did you?"

"They were yella'," Wally said. "And besides, I kept up
with him, didn't I?"

"Just be more careful, Wally. We don't want to be stopped
by the cops."

They followed the Dodge for forty minutes, through the
suburbs and onto a country road.

"Looks like he's headed for Downingtown," Wally said.

"Where's that?"

"It's a little town on the river that was once famous for
moonshining," Wally had a grin on his face as if he knew this
from personal experience. "They hauled malt and sugar in
by boat. When the locals finished their 'shine', they
transported it by river. The federalies made the mistake of
watching the roads."

"Wouldn't the local cops know about the river scam?"

"Hell yes, they knew; they were in on it."

J.C. shook his head.

In a few minutes, they approached Downingtown.

The town was small, once a proud coal-mining town, but
now the old, company shacks stood still, testimony to the
Appalachian reputation.

"He's headed for the Rathskellar," Wally said, slowing
down. "He passed up the only other road that leads out of
town."

Wally downshifted. They crept up the road to the Rathskellar's parking lot. They saw Nicklaus standing on the large lighted front porch of the old, Victorian house that was now a speakeasy and haven for a biker gang. Wally parked the truck at the rear of the large parking lot, keeping the red Dodge and the bar in view. Wally's truck didn't look out of place as there were many other old pickups plus a number of motorcycles in the lot as well.

"What'll we do now?" Wally asked. "Should we go in or wait here?"

"What's that smell?" J.C. asked, screwing up his face in a contemptuous frown. The carbonic acid in the soft drinks had acted as a catalyst on the hard boiled eggs and pepperoni sticks and had now produced enough gas in Wally's intestinal tract to fuel a small village. *Mistake number three.* J.C. jumped out of the truck. "I guess we're going in."

Herman Nicklaus had already entered the bar. Only a few bikers remained on the porch. They sat on the edge of their chairs staring at the two strangers as they walked up the steps. Wally opened the door and stepped in. J.C. followed. There was no retreating now; they were already in. The loud banter that could be heard from outside stopped. Men at the bar swiveled around on their stools to look at the unfamiliar faces. The only sound heard in the bar was made by subtle body movements against leather jackets or chaps. The pool players stopped, their cues held at port arms. Two men were at the jukebox picking songs, their arms wrapped around each other. The bar was dimly lit and most of the patrons were dressed in black. Pastel lights shone over the white, bald, heads that resembled a field of mushrooms.

On closer inspection, J.C. noticed the men had tattoos, ones reflecting Germany's darkest days as well as beards, spiked wristbands and boots. He also noticed only two seats were available—at the very end of the bar. J.C. nudged Wally and they started on their journey toward the empty seats. J.C. led the way, picking his way through the crowd, nudging bodies covered with leather and looking at all the bearded faces. He was thinking of the Burt Reynolds' movie "The Longest Yard" when he heard Wally speak.

"Have you seen my puppy?" J.C. turned to see Wally holding up one of the "lost dog" posters and a leash.

A burly, bearded man stood up; his frail friend started an annoying grin. "What's his name?"

"Adolf," Wally answered without hesitation. *Happy mistake number one.*

"Give that man a drink," the man said amidst cheers of approval. The sea of bodies parted leaving a clear path to the two empty seats at the end of the bar. The bartender began serving J.C. and Wally what would be an assembly line of drinks.

The bodies that had separated when Wally and J.C. entered now paired off. Drinks were hoisted and everyone was having fun, including Wally, who forgot he was on surveillance. The big, burly, bearded guy had his arm around Wally; his frail friend looked disgusted.

After a number of drinks, Wally began telling dirty jokes to his audience. J.C. thought he had better get him out of there before he started his repertoire of gay jokes. *Almost mistake number four.*

"We'd better start looking for Adolf," J.C. said. "He might be hungry."

"What?" Wally asked. "What are you—,"

J.C. grabbed Wally by the arm, said their apologies, and led Wally out of the bar.

Wally staggered through the parking lot to the truck. J.C. helped him into the cab.

"Jason Saxberg's murder was a hate crime," J.C. said.

"Yeah he hated him enough to murder him."

"Jason was sexually mutilated," J.C. said. "A gay wouldn't

have done it. The murderer wasn't gay; he was someone who hated gays."

"I see your point. These are nice guys. I like 'em. Maybe a jilted lover would react in the same manner. Can't we go back and have another drink?"

J.C. thought Wally might have a point, and then dismissed it. "We've had enough fun; we're going to have to get serious from now on. This is too important to be pissing around drinking and telling jokes.

Wally bowed his head. "You're right. What's next?"

"We'll hit Restivo tomorrow," J.C. said, "and I'll have Barb prepare some decent food for us."

"Okay, and I'll bring water and a couple of pee bottles."

Chapter 10

The day of the reverend's funeral should have been bright and warm; after all it was the middle of July. It was anything but. A northwester brought a slow, but steady, rain to Greenville Memorial Cemetery. When the cold raindrops hit the sun-warmed tombstones, they produced steamy, specter-like apparitions that rose steadily toward the sky.

Although the hearse arrived first, the Smith family waited with the casket until the visitors and bishop were in place. The United Methodist Church provided six old pallbearers; their faces strained and their scrawny legs trembled as they marched incongruously to carry the metal casket that encased the stocky reverend. Abigail and her children followed the slow-moving procession.

"Anything new on the case?" a whispered voice said from behind Paul. A big, black dripping umbrella and a Jimmy Cagney floppy fedora almost concealed the man's face.

Paul looked over his left shoulder. "Hi Ted," Theodore Martinet, a city councilman, and classmate of Paul's. "No, nothing yet."

"Is there a problem?" Ted cupped his cigarette to keep it dry.

Paul didn't want to chitchat with anyone. His head pounded from an overindulgence of Bellows, and his sinuses were adding to his discomfort due to the weather. "We're in the process of interviewing the family. There's not much evidence and they're too shook up to remember any pertinent facts."

"Who's your prime suspect?"

"We're still investigating. Too soon to go locking people up."

"I know the department and the mayor are politically motivated," Ted said. "If you do have a suspect, I could file the complaint with the magistrate?"

"Well I don't, not yet. Anyway, an assistant district attorney has to approve a private citizen's complaint before it can proceed. Do you have evidence that would convince him?"

"No, not yet. But I've heard rumors that the reverend was abusive toward kids."

"What! You're kidding," Paul said.

"I'm going to look into it." Ted walked off toward the reverend's family hunched under his umbrella.

Paul thought Ted a little odd, but wondered about what he had said. He focused his attention on the funeral. He would talk to Ted later.

Abigail and her brood followed the casket to the burial site. The bishop, sheltered by a large golf umbrella, praised the reverend's accomplishments throughout his long and illustrious career. The family stood stoic, even when the bishop said he was especially proud of the reverend's participation in many district meetings, annual conferences and missionary conferences held throughout the years.

"That's when he went on his gambling junkets," Martinet whispered in Paul's ear as he made another pass through the crowd.

Paul darted after him, and grabbed his shoulder. "Whoa, Ted. What do you mean?"

Ted cupped a hand around his mouth and lowered his voice. "Just what I said. When the reverend went to his religious meetings and retreats, his extracurricular activities were in the evenings at nearby towns such as Atlantic City. I heard he even used disguises to keep from being recognized."

Ted walked to his car and drove off, leaving Paul thinking about a motive for the reverend's death. He walked back to the gravesite wondering about the possibilities. Was it for gambling debts? Did Reverend Smith gamble around the city? He thought it was worth looking into.

After the prayers, roses were placed of on the casket and the family and visitors departed in the ever-increasing mist.

#

J.C. and Wally were making plans for the surveillance of Jimmy Restivo when Paul walked into the bar. "How was the funeral?" Wally asked.

Paul shook off his trench coat. "Chilly and wet as hell this morning. Give me a beer and a double bourbon."

J.C., who had already poured the beer when he saw Paul walk in, reached for Paul's favorite bottle and topped off a shot glass.

"How's the Saxberg case going?" Wally asked.

"Real slow," Paul said, throwing down the Bellows, followed by a swig of beer. "We've got patrolmen still canvassing the area, talking to people and looking for leads."

"It's kind of early for that stuff, isn't it?" Wally said, frowning as he pointed to the empty shot glass.

"What about a motive?" J.C. asked, trying to break the tense atmosphere.

"Someone probably didn't like fudge packers," Paul said, matter-of-factly. "We've talked to a lot of people and no one had a bad word to say about him. He wasn't a troublemaker, no gang affiliation or drugs. He was just a normal, likable kid."

J.C. looked down at the bar. He couldn't forget the fact that he wouldn't be there if it wasn't for Jason Saxberg pulling him away from that swollen creek the last day of his former life. His stomach knotted up. He grabbed a can of ginger ale and popped the top, swigging hard on it, relieving his tension and the queasiness in his stomach. "He wasn't the kind to impose himself on anybody. Why'd someone have to kill him—especially that way?"

"We'll get him, eventually," Paul said. "We usually do."

"I'd like to have five minutes alone with the guy when you catch up with him." J.C. said. "I'd like to talk to him."

Wally cleared his throat. "Like you talked to that big ex-navy guy last year?"

"He had it coming," J.C. said. "Shouldn't have hit that young girl."

"After he tried to sucker-punch you, he didn't get a punch near you," Wally said, motioning to Paul, his fists flailing. "I never saw anything like it, just like that Kane guy on television, you know, the Kung-Fu show."

"I heard about that," Paul said. "Maybe you were a martial artist before you lost your memory, or a bodyguard or something. That ability doesn't come naturally; you relied on your reflexes. You might have been trained for martial arts."

"Are there places I can check if my hands are registered?" J.C. asked, and then remembered what Commander Albright had told him. "I'll let Commander Albright know about this. He always said to let him know if he could help. He could check with martial arts associations or something, maybe send my picture around."

"Good idea," Paul and Wally said in unison.

Wally was still focused on getting more information about the Saxberg case. He turned to Paul. "What about his friends? Did your detectives come up with anything? What about that skinhead guy?"

"How do you know about that?" Paul asked. "Have you two Sherlocks been snooping around?"

"Just heard talk in the bar, that's all," J.C. said. "I was just telling Wally about it." He shot a look at Wally.

"They're a harmless bunch—those skinheads," Paul said. "They only pretend to be the real thing. Image, you know— they attract spoiled rich kids, kids with low self-esteem, weaklings trying to look tough. It's an invented lifestyle for them. They accept each other and want others to fear them. They're a bunch of pussies."

"No other friends then," Wally asked. "No suspects?"

"Not yet," Paul said, looking each man in the eye, "but the police will handle it, understood?"

"Absolutely," J.C. said, followed by a quick "Right," from Wally.

Paul left.

"What time tonight?" Wally asked.

"Six o'clock."

"Why so early?

"Services start at seven o'clock at the church," J.C. said. "We'll want to see who he associates with and where he goes, right?"

"Right."

"Bring Paul's camcorder."

"I've already picked it up."

Chapter 11

Wally strutted into Ducheck's at 5:50, ten minutes early. He was wearing a dark suit, black patent leather shoes and a black beret. He had a camcorder case strapped around his neck; he was ready for the Restivo surveillance.

J.C. stopped washing glasses and dried his hands. "I see you didn't forget the camcorder. How about the drinks and the pee bottles?

"Two of them," Wally said, holding up two wide-mouth plastic juice bottles. "Mine and yours. How about the snacks? You didn't bring eggs and pepperoni, did you?"

J.C. reached under the bar and grabbed a lunch bucket. He opened the lid. "No, Barb made us tuna salad sandwiches before she left for work. Let's see . . . Oreo cookies and chips too."

Nuggets walked into the bar. J.C. had asked him to be available at 6:00 p.m. "Where you guys off to?"

"We're going to see a friend of Jason's," J.C. said. "Maybe he can give us some information."

Nuggets looked at the bag strapped around Wally's neck. "Are you going to videotape the conversation?"

"Maybe we can catch him in a compromising position," Wally said, hiking up his pants with his thumbs, like a two-bit country sheriff. "We're on a surveillance too."

"Good luck," Nuggets said, taking his place behind the bar.

Wally and J.C. grabbed their remaining gear and left. They stowed the equipment in Wally's truck and drove to McKee Avenue on the north central part of town near the 36th Street Park. This was the residential part of town forty years ago. Old money created the area, but it had moved to the suburbs years ago. They parked across the street from the church.

"What's the name of this church?" Wally asked.

"Fundamentalist Bible Fellowship Church. It's a remodeled jewelry shop that was donated by a philanthropist."

The building was a wide two-storey building on a corner lot. The facade of the first floor was flagstone; the second floor was covered in asbestos shingles. Plywood, painted gray, covered the former, large display windows. The second-storey windows were also covered with plywood, giving the building an aura of secrecy.

Wally shifted in his seat. "How'd you know all this?"

"Bar talk."

Wally re-capped his beret. "What do you mean bar talk?"

"You know Ten Quarts Petty, don't you?" Wally nodded, raising his eyebrows. J.C. continued. "He knows everything and everybody, right? Well, this afternoon, he was the only one in the bar. So instead of him busting my chops with his one-sided conversation, I started my own agenda."

Wally's lips slowly formed a grin. "I see where you're going with this."

"Right. I led him on to the subject of religion, which gave him the pulpit for a fifteen minute dissertation, and then I casually dropped the name Tony Restivo."

"Clever. Then you sat back and listened."

J.C. opened the cooler and retrieved a bottle of water. "I learned more about the Restivo family than I really wanted to know. I had to butt in to ask about Jimmy."

"I really don't like to be around Ten Quarts," Wally said, waving his hand dismissively, "but he is very knowledgeable about a lot of subjects in general, and a lot of people in particular. What did he tell you about this church?"

"He said it was one of the churches that fell under the category of what is known as fundamentalist. Fire and brimstone, the vengeful God, fear and punishment—things like that."

"A very controlling religion," Wally mused, stroking his chin. "Must be very strict."

They looked at each other. J.C. spoke first. "Maybe we can be the Devil's advocate? I've noticed that the ultra religious usually have something to hide. I'll bet Jimmy Restivo is no exception. Does Paul's camcorder have the feature that displays the time and date on it?"

Wally padded the camcorder case and smiled. "Sure does. It'll come in handy on replay."

Jimmy Restivo arrived at 6:50 in a gray Buick Century. J.C. recognized him from a picture he had seen at Mrs. Saxberg's house. Jimmy parked on a side street, next to the church's parking lot. Wally then walked along the sidewalk and into the building. Wally recorded Jimmy's entrance. He backed the truck into an empty lot across from the church. They were now facing all possible avenues of departure.

"Did you get the license number on the video?" J.C. asked.

Wally re-wound the tape and pressed play. He viewed what was recorded on the flip-out screen. "No, I didn't get it."

"I'll wait a while, walk up to the lot, and tape it," J.C. said. "We want to make sure we document everything." They each ate a tuna sandwich and swigged water as they waited. J.C. used the camcorder to capture Jimmy leaving the church at 8:30.

Wally waited until Jimmy had a half-block lead before he started to follow him. He was more careful this time with the red lights. They followed him west, through town, and onto Route 84. Jimmy turned onto the interstate. He increased his speed to 65 m.p.h.

Twenty minutes later, he crossed the border into West Virginia. "Looks like he's going to Wheeling," J.C. said.

They stayed far enough in back to keep him in sight. Another fifteen minutes went by.

"I have to pee," Wally said. "I can't go in the bottle and drive at the same time."

"What do you want me to do? Hold it for you?"

Wally shot a glance, "You can grab the steering wheel."

J.C. was thinking. "Can't it wait for a while? We're coming into Wheeling."

Jimmy drove to the southeast section of the city in an area scheduled for redevelopment. He pulled into a grassy parking lot off Sutter Street and walked toward a brick, one-storey building. The large, red neon sign above the door identified it as the "Gayiety." It was 9:45. J.C. documented the event with the camcorder. A truck stop was 200 yards away, south of the bushes where Wally was relieving himself.

Wally joined J.C. in the truck. "This kid doesn't know us from Adam, does he?"

They looked at each other. J.C. looked at the camcorder case. "Can you record with the camcorder in the case?"

Wally grabbed the case. "I think so," he said reaching for his stainless steel pocketknife. He cut a round hole at the lens end of the case. He slipped the camera back in and checked its position. "Yep, sure can. I don't think Paul will mind." He then cut a flap at the rear of the case for access to the eyepiece and controls.

J.C. took the camera. They walked toward the Gayiety. They could hear laughter and an occasional vociferous roar from inside.

The Gayiety was the modern version of a burlesque

theatre, except all the clothes of the dancers came off and audience participation was encouraged. Some men had left their tables and were crowding near the stage. They jabbed dead presidents in the air, hoping to get the attention of the dancer, so they could stuff bills in a G-string or a fleshy crevice.

J.C. felt guilty about being in a strip joint while the only woman in his life was working. He had to find the person who murdered Jason to find his own identity and the possibility of a future with Barb. He scanned the area leaving any guilt behind.

Off to the right stretched the bar, jammed with men pointing at the stage, laughing, some bent over in hysterics. A few women, almost hidden by the multitude of men, were seated at the bar or at tables, hustling drinks. The patrons whooped in laughter when a dancer grabbed a fin or a ten-spot from a customer and let them grope, feel or sometimes kiss a body part.

Through the smoke-filled crowd, J.C. spotted Jimmy at a table at the far end of the room. He was ordering a drink. Wally and J.C. picked their way through the throng and found a table that provided a good view. Wally ordered drinks from one of the scantily clad waitresses. J.C. positioned the camcorder case on the table and checked its field of view. J.C. waited until the waitress brought Jimmy his mixed drink. Then he hit the start button and let the camcorder capture Jimmy placing a bill in the waitress' cleavage.

"Did you get that?" Wally asked.

J.C. sat back in his chair and smiled. "Absolutely."

In the next twenty minutes, Jimmy ordered two more mixed drinks. He reached in his wallet and took out a twenty. He stood up and started for the stage.

"Start the camcorder," Wally said. "Those drinks got him horny; he's about to do something stupid."

J.C. adjusted the camcorder for a wider shot to include the big-breasted dancer. There must have been fifteen men at the front of the stage, jockeying for position, stabbing fives and tens into the air, trying to get the dancer's attention. Jimmy joined them. He held up a Jackson. The dancer spotted Jimmy's twenty and jogged to a position in front of him. With her perfect eyesight, Jimmy thought, she could probably spot a nickel at thirty yards.

The woman jiggled a little dance in front of Jimmy. He waved the twenty again. She walked closer to him. Jimmy started to put the bill in her g-string.

"You getting all this," Wally asked.

"Every little jiggle."

Jimmy hesitated about stuffing the twenty in the dancer's g-string and asked her a question. She knelt down on the two-foot stage, pulled her g-string aside and Jimmy dove in, head first. The crowd erupted in a roar of whistles, hoots and hollers. The woman grabbed Jimmy's greenback, shot to her feet and was off dancing again, looking for another large denomination bill.

"Did you get that?" Wally asked.

"In living color. I even zoomed in for a close up. She's at the other end of the stage. Let's have a beer."

Wally looked at the dancer, then J.C. He opened his wallet and said, "Do you have a spare twenty?"

J.C. smacked his arm. Wally smiled.

Jimmy finished his fourth drink and went to the bar. He bought a woman a drink. She was a pretty brunette wearing a low-cut blue blouse and tight, white slacks. She smiled and put her arm around him. They talked and giggled as they finished their drinks. When they stood up to leave, Wally commented she was a head taller than Jimmy and heavier too.

Wally and J.C. followed the couple into the parking lot. Jimmy opened his car door for his chubby new friend and grabbed her butt as she got in.

"Isn't he cavalier?" J.C. said, as he recorded the event.

Jimmy drove to a residential area ten minutes away and parked in front of a two-storey brick house. The couple walked up a stone path to the door. As Wally drove by, J.C. taped the duo entering the house. Wally then drove around the block and parked a few houses away. J.C. was taping the house when the upstairs light came on. It was 11:05. J.C. continued taping. At 11:08, the lights went off.

"I'll keep taping," J.C. said. "We want an accurate documentation of the times."

"Yeah, it shouldn't be long anyway. He's as hot as a firecracker."

At 11:11 the lights came on again. Four minutes later, at 11:15 they went off. Jimmy left the house at 11:17.

Wally and J.C. followed Jimmy out of Wheeling and onto Route 84.

"Looks like he's going home." Wally said.

"Doesn't matter where he's going now. He gave us what we wanted."

"If Jimmy Restivo has any information about the Saxberg murder, this tape will pry it out of him."

Chapter 12

Gerri slid, a few inches at a time, over the old and cracked Naugahyde seat, stopping each time to flick crumb minutiae off the bench with a long, pointed fingernail. Paul alternately adjusted his tie and hiked up his pants while standing at the edge of the booth. Gerri finally slumped into a depression created by the seat's decrepit springs and maundered a barely audible complaint as she jostled her alligator purse into position at her side. Paul slid into the booth in one fluid motion and motioned to Nuggets for service.

J.C. sat down across from them at the semicircular table. It was Saturday and Paul had just picked up Gerri and had expected to find Wally at Ducheck's. It was Wally's birthday and they were going to take him out to dinner.

"He's usually here at this time, isn't he?" Gerri asked. "What could be keeping him?"

"He'll be here any minute," J.C. knew Wally was at Paul's house making a copy of the Restivo tape.

At that very moment, Wally had just hooked up the output of Paul's recorder to the input of the recorder he brought from home. He then played the Restivo tape on

Paul's recorder and recorded it on his own. It took more time than he figured it would. He had to move Paul's TV stand, being careful not to leave evidence of his visit there. Paul would ask a lot of questions as to why he was secretly dubbing a tape, especially if he found out the tape was of Jimmy Restivo.

Back at the bar, Paul was looking at his watch as their drinks arrived. "We have a six o'clock reservation for dinner and I'm getting hungry."

Nuggets poured a Perrier for Gerri and carefully placed a double in front of Paul. The empty shot-glass and the draft that Nuggets placed on the table hit simultaneously. Gerri nervously shook the ice cubes in her glass as she stared at the empty two-ounce vessel.

"You've got plenty of time," J.C. said. "Tell me, how was the reverend's funeral?"

Paul talked about the lousy weather, the people in attendance and how the bishop had paid his respects to the reverend by complimenting his attendance at various meetings and seminars.

Then Paul leaned forward, looked around to see if anyone was listening and said, "Don't repeat this, but I heard from a reliable source that the reverend was a little too liberal about his teaching procedures."

"What do you mean?" J.C. asked.

Gerri made faces into a compact, touching up her makeup. "Sounds like child molesting to me," she said matter-of-factly.

J.C. leaned forward, his eyebrows arched into his forehead, creating ruts. "No way. I mean that's mind blowing." He held his temples with his hands, looked away, then back at Paul. "Any truth to that?"

"I don't know, but it's worth looking into. Could be a motive for murder. I also found out that the reverend liked to gamble. He used religious retreats and seminars as a way to get away from home for gaming. He even used disguises."

"I thought your only suspects were limited to the reverend's family," J.C. said.

Paul looked J.C. in the eye, hesitated, then said in a knowing tone, "If I find out that the reverend did abuse young boys, what would stop him from abusing his own?"

"Holy shit. I didn't think of that," J.C. said.

"It's a consideration." Paul looked hard at Gerri and J.C. "This has to be kept confidential, understand?" They nodded.

"It's a shame, isn't it?" Gerri said. "Abuse is such a terrible thing, especially by a reverend. It's an abuse of power, an abuse of privilege."

J.C. slowly shook his head. "It's really hard to believe."

"Not real hard," Paul said, looking at Gerri. "We witnessed it twice last week."

"Twice?" Gerri asked.

"Yeah, the family at Rotolo's Restaurant—"

"Oh, I saw that," Gerri said. "Everyone in the restaurant did. The way that man hit his son; it was terrible. When was the other one?"

"At the park," Paul said. He looked at Gerri to see if she remembered. She looked puzzled.

"The yuppie couple. They were playing badminton—"

"What, that wasn't abuse."

"Absolutely, It wasn't physical abuse like we witnessed at Rotolo's. It was emotional abuse."

J.C.'s expression revealed that he understood what Paul had said.

"Maybe Barb can find out if the reverend's kids were abused." Paul was confused.

"She has a friend who works in the records department at the hospital."

"Good idea," Paul said. "I can't subpoena their records yet. It's privileged information. I'm going to talk with Matthew's supervisor first. That'll give Barb's friend some time before I talk to Ruth's supervisor."

"Great, I'll call her tonight." J.C. looked pleased with himself, then asked, "How's the Saxberg case coming? Do you have any suspects?"

"Are you still hyped-up on that case?"

"I can't help it," J.C. answered. "He saved my life. I owe him. I want to see the bastard who—"

"You could get hurt," Paul said. "You don't know what you're dealing with here. If you had seen what was done to him, you'd think twice about getting involved. We're dealing with an extremely hateful person here—"

"That's just it," J.C. said. "The same hateful animals that did that to Jason might just feel the same way about me."

Gerri cocked her head and at the same time, lowering it slightly and looked at him in a questioning manner.

"Jason and I were both ostracized by the community," J.C. said. "He, for being gay, and me for having a dubious past—a past that included unexplained multiple gunshot wounds."

"But people see you for what you are," Gerri said. "They know you by now. It's been what . . . three years?"

"Did they know Jason?" J.C.'s face knotted in disgust. "He was in his twenties. Did they know him? From what we just heard, did people really know Reverend Smith? People hate and despise people for the wrong reasons. That's why I have to get involved. I have a connection to Jason Saxberg."

"Your problem is that you don't know who you are," Paul said. "Wally mentioned the other day that you were going to look into martial arts organizations. How's that going?"

J.C.'s facial expression changed from disgust to hope. "I'm compiling a list of organizations in the four-state area. I'm going to give it to Commander Albright to check out."

"Good luck." Paul was about to order another drink when Wally walked in. "There's the birthday boy. What kept you?"

"Traffic," Wally said, shooting a wink at J.C. "It's murder out there. Is everyone ready? What's the hold-up? I'm hungry."

They all got up to leave and walked toward the bar. J.C. caught Wally's eye. "See you later?"

"Yeah, around eight. I want to watch that movie with Gina Lottabody." Wally smiled as he turned to walk out.

#

J.C. liked the way the old Bronco handled. The new brakes and wheel alignment made it feel three years younger. Wally rode shotgun as they drove toward Restivo's church. They wanted to confront him about his extracurricular church activities and use it as leverage to get information about the Saxberg case. "So, how was dinner?" J.C. asked.

"Great, I had ravioli. Paul and Gerri had penné."

"Did Paul and Gerri sing 'Happy Birthday' to you?"

"No, but the waitress brought me a piece of cake."

"That was awful nice of her," J.C. said. "Who told her it was your birthday, Paul or Gerri?"

"She thought I was cute."

J.C. knew what Wally had done. "You told her."

Wally's sheepish look gave him away, and then he smiled. "When Gerri was in the powder room and Paul went to the bar for another round of drinks, I may have mentioned it."

J.C. laughed as he made a left turn. "At least you didn't tell her to bring the waiter and cooking staff out to sing to you,"

"She said they were busy," Wally laughed, then his face got serious. "Commander Albright came in with his wife. They were dressed to kill. Gerri said Mrs. Albright's dress was very expensive."

"Did they sit near you?"

"No, the maître d' sat them at what appeared to be their usual table. Paul talked to him though; you know how it is. He couldn't shun the commander."

"No, I guess that would be an insult."

"That's how bureaucracy works," Wally said. "But, he managed to talk to him about the list you're compiling on martial arts organizations. He thinks it's a great idea."

They arrived at the church at 8:15, expecting Jimmy to leave at 8:30. They found his gray Buick Century parked close to a newer Jaguar. J.C. parked facing Jimmy's car, almost against his bumper. He didn't want to provide Jimmy an easy exit.

The last rays of sunlight were disappearing when Jimmy Restivo sauntered out of the church, and headed for his car. Wally and J.C. got out of the Bronco and met him on the sidewalk.

"Jimmy Restivo?" Wally asked.

"Yes," he said, looking first at Wally, then at J.C. "Can I help you?"

"You certainly can," J.C. said. "We'd like to talk to you about the Saxberg murder."

"What," Jimmy said. "I don't know what the hell—" he looked around to see if anyone was within earshot. He turned to face J.C. "I don't know anything about that murder."

He started to walk toward his car, but Wally cut him off. "Excuse me. Maybe we should explain why we want to talk to you."]

Jimmy looked at both of them. "Are you the police?"

"No," Wally said, pointing at J.C., "but he's a private detective."

"I don't have to talk to him," he said, waving his arm dismissively.

"Maybe you want to talk to me then," Wally said.

"Who the hell are you, old man?"

"I'm president of the local chapter of The Muff-diver's Association."

Jimmy's facial expression changed from puzzlement to fright. He looked around again to see if anyone was in earshot. "Why . . . what do . . . do you mean?"

J.C. had taken the camcorder from the Bronco. He held it up and opened the hinged viewing door. "This is what we mean." J.C. started the tape and showed Jimmy the excerpt with the most leverage—Jimmy eating at the "Y."

Jimmy's jaw dropped as he gazed at his image on the screen. He reached for the camcorder. J.C. snatched it from his grasp.

"Where . . . where did you get that. That's illegal."

"No it isn't," Wally said. "The Gayiety is a public bar. There were no signs about cameras. Ask your father."

Jimmy's jaw dropped; his head slumped. "What do you guys want?"

"We want to talk about what you know about the Saxberg murder," J.C. said.

"I don't know anything," Jimmy replied.

"You'd better know something," Wally said, "or this little harlequinade will be played in front of your congregation."

J.C. looked at Wally. Wally looked back at J.C. with an expression of "what?" on his face.

Jimmy's lip quivered, the corners of his mouth turned down and he was on the verge of crying.

J.C. heard voices getting closer. He looked toward the church and saw a man in black and two others coming toward them, chatting and joking as they walked.

"Hello reverend," Jimmy said. He looked relieved.

"Jimmy? Is that you?" the minister said. His head jutted forward, his eyes squinting behind small, round eyeglasses.

"Yes sir, I was just . . . talking to . . . ah . . . my friends."

The reverend looked Wally and J.C. over as if they were convicted felons. His friends did the same. "I'll walk you to your car, James," he said, putting his arm around Jimmy's shoulder, "Service is early tomorrow you know. You've got to get your sleep."

J.C. pointed a finger toward Jimmy. "I'll see you tomorrow. We have to talk."

Jimmy opened his mouth to speak, but the reverend stifled him by raising his hand. "After service, we're going to retreat; he'll be getting home very late."

Wally stared at the reverend. "You got services or retreats every day?"

The reverend pulled back his head and looked Wally over as if trying to sense his essence. "No, of course not."

Wally turned his gaze to Jimmy. "We'll see you later then."

The reverend and his friends ushered Jimmy to his car. One of the men got in his Jaguar and left. Wally and J.C. watched Jimmy drive off.

"We can catch him Monday," Wally said.

"Not Monday, I've scheduled an appointment at the community college. I'm meeting with an advisor at seven o'clock for some computer courses."

"Yeah, I remember. That'll be fine," Wally said. "We'll talk to him Tuesday then."

They got in Wally's truck. J.C. turned to Wally. "Harlequinade?"

Chapter 13

Westchester County Community College is located in Arden, a small rural town, fifty-five miles north of Greenville. The town is ensconced on a plateau in the Oneidas, a small, old mountain range between sprawling hills and valleys.

The campus consists of nine, low profile, brick buildings, except for the high-domed auditorium, two athletic fields, and various parking lots, all spread over a well-manicured 135 acres. Science and technology is the specialty of the college followed closely by the popular culinary arts program.

J.C.parked near the administration building in parking lot "A." He walked across the asphalt lot, dodging vehicles that were leaving after the 6:00 p.m. Monday classes. A secretary directed him to Warner Hall, the adjoining building that housed the computer science department.

J.C. quickly found the advisor's office. A bald man waved him in and explained the associate degree program in computer technology. He said it was a four-semester course of study that covered math, science, the humanities, microcomputer and applications software, computer operations, hypermedia and cal information structures, plus others for a total of sixty-six credits.

J.C. explained he wanted basic courses on the computer and the Internet. The bald man described the non-credit computer courses that provided leisure and recreational activities for the public. He handed over a pamphlet that listed a prospectus for each course. J.C. found a vacant room, sat at a desk and mulled over the selection of courses. He decided to take "Intro to the Internet" and "Intro to Windows 98/XP." He figured he could handle both at the same time. "Using a Scanner and Digital Camera" would come later.

J.C. glanced in classrooms as he toured the building. He was excited about being a student, an experience he was sure he once had, but couldn't remember. After J.C. had a bite to eat at the snack bar, a student directed him to a room where an "Intro to Windows" class was being taught. J.C.'s excitement grew as he listened to the instructor explaining how to cut and paste selected blocks of words in a document. It seemed easy for J.C. and he wondered if he had ever taken a course on computers before. Before he knew it, the class was over and it was time for him to leave. J.C. left feeling a sense of accomplishment. It was dark as he drove off campus and headed home.

J.C. headed south, driving sixty-five miles an hour on the flat, straight, four-lane highway. This soon changed however, as he reached the edge of the plateau and started to descend the hilly, old mountain. It became darker as he drove below the Oneidas peaks and mounds. Fog had descended down from the valleys of the hills he had just driven through, making visibility harder. He decreased his speed, even more so on the curves.

Traffic was light this time of night. Commuters between Greenville and Monaco, an industrial town ten miles north of Arden were home hours ago. J.C. was taking his time, listening to light rock on FM 96.1, his favorite station.

J.C. didn't notice a dark-colored truck coming up behind him. The truck edged up alongside, but didn't pass. It stayed even with the Bronco until he glanced over and noticed that the driver was wearing a ski mask. J.C. was startled. He glanced straight ahead to make sure he was on the road and then back again at the driver in the dark truck. The masked driver was looking at him. J.C. could tell from the floppy opening in the man's mask that he was smiling.

When J.C. turned his attention back to the road, the truck rammed the side of the Bronco with a loud metallic crash, jarring J.C.'s head into the doorpost. He was almost knocked unconscious; he tried to keep the vehicle under control. The Bronco veered to the right, off the road onto the berm. It bounced on weathered ruts and kicked up pebbles that pinged off its chrome bumpers and the wheel-wells. J.C. quickly regained control and pulled back onto the road. He was lucky, the berm here was wide enough for a recovery; for most of the highway, it was much narrower or petered off into tall grass and shrubs. The forest loomed in the background.

The truck tried to ram him again, but J.C. was ready this time. He cut to the left, hitting the truck, negating its force. The truck swerved left, preparing to cut back into the Bronco's side, but J.C. countered his move again. He watched the driver's face; he wasn't smiling anymore. The truck kept even with the Bronco. J.C. noticed the driver lean over toward the passenger seat and grab something. Suddenly he had something shiny in his hand.

Oh my god, it's a gun.

The masked driver pointed the gun at J.C. and fired. J.C. saw the man's movement and instinctively jammed his foot on the brake and leaned his head back. He saw the flame from the gun's barrel rush toward him and heard its report. The bullet blasted through his side window and exited at the upper right corner of the windshield. Shards of glass covered the dash and seats. J.C. wiped some from his face.

J.C.'s car was now slightly in back and to the right of the truck. He floored the accelerator and turned to the left, hitting the truck in the right rear. The truck lurched forward, swaying a little as if the driver was trying to keep it under control. That's all J.C. needed to see. He plowed into the rear of the truck, knocking it forward again. It swerved again. He thought if he could hit it as it was swaying, he could force it off the road.

He figured if he could hit the truck, then floor it as he quickly downshifted, he would have enough speed and power to hit the truck as it was swaying. He saw the masked man raise his right arm over the front seat of the truck. He still had the gun in his hand. J.C. reacted. He rammed the back of the truck as the man fired off a round. It went astray, through the windshield on the passenger side of the Bronco. J.C. floored the accelerator and a moment later, downshifted. As the truck's rear end swerved left, the Bronco pitched forward striking the truck in the right rear.

The truck spun around in a cloud of blue smoke and screeching tires. It left the highway, shot across the narrow berm and slid through the grass. J.C. watched the beam from the truck's headlights bounce up and down on the forested growth of a nearby hillside as the truck spun through the shrubbery. The bouncing beams stopped. The truck had stopped.

J.C. didn't wait around to see if the truck recovered, but sped off down the mountain, slowing only on curves. He was unarmed and didn't want to take a chance with the man in the ski mask.

Who wants to kill me? J.C. wondered if it was the same person who had tried three years ago when Jason interceded. What about the attempt made on his life when his brakes failed coming down a similar mountain two years ago. Was he really out of brake fluid? Could Jimmy Restivo be responsible? They were supposed to meet the following night. Did he have something to hide that was important enough to kill for? Surely the tape that he and Wally recorded didn't warrant murder. But Jimmy was a religious nut. Nothing was more important to these people than their pious image. J.C. didn't know who his enemies were, and didn't know where to look—past Jimmy Restivo, that is.

The wind that blew in the shattered windows awakened a new fear in J.C. How was he going to explain the bullet holes in his Bronco? People were suspicious enough about the bullet wounds in his body. He thought he'd call Wally in the morning. But what if the assassin knew where he lived? Where could he go? It was getting late. He didn't want to bother anyone at this hour. J.C. drove to Wally's and decided to park in his back yard. He drove down the long driveway, across the manicured lawn and parked near Wally's pigeon coop. He was exhausted and fell asleep instantly.

#

J.C. had forgotten about the injury to his head when he was rammed—that is until he woke up the next morning.

He sat there, leaning against the door, his head throbbing as if a blacksmith's hammer was pounding on it. He was afraid to move, afraid to open his eyes, not just because of his suffering, but because of what he might see. He didn't want to see the antiseptic whiteness of a hospital again. He couldn't stand the thought of starting all over again.

His eyes twitched. The large, dark maroon and midnight-blue splotches of color inside his eyelids were replaced by dark reds, then orange, the color getting lighter and brighter, making his head throb even more. He finally opened his swollen and bloodshot eyes to see a familiar scene. He was happy; he was in Wally's backyard, under a large pin oak next to a decrepit pigeon coop. He hadn't lost his memory again. It was a day to celebrate, he thought, but then he remembered. What about the man who tried to kill him?

He was enveloped with pain. The flutter of pigeons jockeying for position in the coop made him tremble with fear. He stiffened in the seat and clutched the steering wheel. It's only a bunch of damn pigeons, he thought. *I can't let this son of a bitch change my life like this. I'll find him if it takes me forever.*

J.C.'s jaw was tight, his lips barely moving, whispering his resolve when Wally came running across the yard.

"What the hell you doin'? Look what you did to my lawn." He was pointing to the ruts in the ground as he walked toward J.C. The Bronco was facing away from Wally. J.C. turned in his seat and looked out the shattered driver's window as Wally approached.

Wally stopped five yards short. "What the hell . . . What happened to your face?" He looked at the broken windows as he walked forward slowly, his arms outstretched questioning, his mouth and eyes open in astonishment. "Are you all right?" He bent forward and touched the ragged hole in the doorframe. "Is this a bullet hole? Christ, what happened?"

J.C. labored to open the door. Wally helped him out. "I've had better days. Someone tried to kill me last night. Have any coffee made?"

Wally helped J.C. to the house, supporting him as they stumbled through the soft, tire-rutted yard.

In the kitchen, over coffee, J.C. explained what happened the night before. Wally was shaken. "Who knew you were going to the college?" Wally asked. "Who'd you talk to?"

J.C. shook his head from side to side. "Someone had to follow me. You and Paul were the only ones that knew where I was going."

Wally scratched his head.

J.C. strained to get up, his muscles cramped by sleeping

in the Bronco. "I'm going to shower and rest up this afternoon. I'll get Nuggets to tend bar." He shuffled to the door.

"Yeah, take it easy," Wally said. "How's your head? Are you sure you're all right?"

"If a bullet to the head didn't stop me, a little bump isn't anything to worry about." J.C. pushed the door open and stopped. "I'll call Jimmy Restivo and set up a meeting for tonight. I'll call you."

#

Barb rinsed the bloodstained cloth in the sink, then soaked it in hot water. She squeezed out the excess, came into the living room and wiped the remaining dried blood from J.C.'s face.

"That's a nasty bump on your head," she said, dabbing antiseptic cream on his facial cuts. "You'll probably need stitches."

Barb comforted J.C., sitting next to him on the couch in his living room. That's what he felt he needed, but had hesitated about calling her. She finished putting the last bandage on his face and ran her fingers through his wavy, sandy blond hair.

J.C. reached up and grabbed her wrist. His soulful eyes evoked sorrow as he spoke. "I think I want to be alone now. I'm sorry, this is hard for me."

"Worrying about your past again?"

J.C. turned and looked out the window. "Yeah, my past. Who knows?"

"I'm not worried about it."

"You should be." His voice got louder and he talked faster, almost in a desperate tone. "What if I'm married? What if I'm an escaped convict?" He stopped momentarily to think, then continued in a solemn voice, "Maybe it could be worse."

"I'll take my chances." Barb smiled and caressed his cheek. "I'm betting on none of the above."

J.C. reached up and pulled her to him; her warmth against his body and her comforting words would chase the demons away temporarily.

They snuggled and talked until Barb looked at her wristwatch and realized it was almost noon. "I have to go. I start early today." She stood up and grabbed her purse from the coffee table.

J.C. sat up halfway, leaning on his left elbow. He didn't want her to go, but he knew she had to go. Watching her beautiful smile and then her wave through the half-closed door cemented his resolve to find Jason's murderer—to find his true identity. He needed to do this not only for himself, but for Barb as well. Jimmy Restivo might be the starting point.

Chapter 14

Wally and J.C. were in Wally's Chevy, headed for an 8:00 p.m. meeting with Jimmy Restivo at a restaurant in the opulent Glenwood Heights section of the city.

"Why didn't you come in the house last night?" Wally asked. "Do you prefer being with my pigeons?"

"I was scared Wally. I didn't know if I was being followed." J.C. shifted in his seat toward Wally. "I didn't want to get you involved. I didn't know what do to; I was shook up."

"Why didn't you go straight to the police station?"

"I figured he'd think I'd go there," J.C. said. "He would've caught up with me in the slow-moving city traffic. I was passing your place, so I pulled in."

Wally nodded as if he understood J.C.'s logic. "Did you catch a glimpse of his face or a plate number?"

"No, I was too busy trying to stay alive."

"Who would want to kill you? Do you think it's the same guy from three years ago? The one that left you for dead?"

"I thought about that all night. I'm not sure. Then I thought about losing my brakes two years ago. Remember that? Was it just a coincidence or was someone trying to kill me then?"

Wally hesitated. "Maybe you've got something there. I didn't think about it at the time, but now that this happened . . . it's possible."

"Well, there's Restivo," J.C. said. "Do you think it could've been him?"

Wally shook his head. "Naw, he's not the type. He's all show, no go."

"You don't think he'd kill someone to protect his image, do you?"

"No, I don't think so," Wally said, waving off the thought with his hand. "Besides, he knows there's two of us and we have copies of the tape. He doesn't know where the tapes are or if we've given them to someone to hold. He'd have to kill us both and we'd have to have the copies on us. He wouldn't take that chance."

"I still don't trust him. I think he'd do almost anything to keep his favorite pastime a secret."

Wally's smile eased J.C.'s doubts. "And that's why we're going to ask him about the Saxberg murder. If he knows something, he'll tell us."

Wally pulled into the spacious restaurant parking lot.

"I've never been here before," J.C. said

Tall pines and fragrant fruit trees framed the cozy restaurant. Smaller shrubs and annuals nestled near the walkways and added a variety of color to the landscape. The split-level building was covered in fieldstone except for its right wing, which was a large, glass-enclosed dining room.

"This is really nice," J.C. said. "I'll have to bring Barb here sometime."

They entered a large foyer. The hostess station was off to the right, near the dining area's stained-glass French doors. To the left a modern, luxurious bar was against the right wall. Tables were to the left against the windows. The place was packed.

J.C. spotted Jimmy Restivo through the human merry-go-round of faces and bodies of customers and busy waitresses. Wally and J.C. made their way through the human obstacle course to the booth at the end of the bar where Jimmy sat fidgeting. Wally and J.C. sat opposite him.

"Do you guys want a ginger ale or mineral water?" Jimmy asked.

Wally leaned toward Jimmy, cupped his hand near his mouth as if trying to keep his words confidential, and shouted, "You don't have to put on an act for us. We know you . . . remember?"

J.C. watched Jimmy's face turn red. "There are a lot of people here. Maybe we should go somewhere else?"

"There's a back room," Jimmy said. "We can talk there." He stood up, walked a few feet to the wall that separated the booth from the bar, and opened a door. Jimmy flipped a light on. The room wasn't spacious, fifteen-foot-square, with four card tables strategically placed throughout.

"They use it for playing cards," Jimmy said. "You know five-hundred bid." He looked for a sign of acknowledgment from Wally and J.C., but got none. "There's a lot of women that play it."

J.C. sat down and motioned to a chair for Jimmy. Wally looked around the room before he took a seat.

"What do you guys want?" Jimmy asked. "Something about Saxberg being murdered?"

As J.C. leaned toward Jimmy, his eyes narrowed. "First of all, I want to know where you were last night."

"Last night? I was home last night. Why?"

"Can you verify it?" J.C. asked, leaning forward again. "Was someone there with you? What were you doing?"

Jimmy started to look frightened. Wally butted in. "All my friend wants to know is what you were doing last night and with whom."

Jimmy thought for a moment. "I watched the Pirates last night. Why do you want to know?"

"What was the score?" Wally asked.

"Three-two, Philly."

Wally nodded to J.C.

J.C. slid back in his chair. "What we want," he said, "is information on the Saxberg murder."

Jimmy Restivo opened his arms and stretched out his hands, palms up. "I don't know a thing about his murder. I hardly knew him."

"You knew him," Wally said. "You went to the funeral home, didn't you?"

J.C. interrupted. "You went to school with him too. Don't give us that line of crap that you didn't know him."

"I swear. I don't know anything about his murder." Jimmy's facial contortions reflected his pleading for understanding.

Wally grabbed Jimmy's shoulder. "Then you know someone who does. Give us a name."

"I don't know who would be involved. Honest—"

Wally said calmly, "No name, no tapes. We'll give a copy to reverend . . . What's his name, J.C.?"

"Okay, okay," Jimmy said. "Let me think a little."

Wally nodded and smiled.

J.C. knew Restivo was going to talk. He felt this information would be the first step in garnering some evidence that would shed light on the Saxberg murder. J.C.'s commitment became stronger.

"The only person I can think of that might know something about Jason's murder is Ralph Fleming," Jimmy said.

"Who's Ralph Fleming?" J.C. asked.

"I think he deals drugs. He's always around; he knows everybody. I saw him with a group of guys by the park about a week before Jason's murder. Jason was there."

"Why him?" Wally asked. "Jason was probably around a lot of people before he was murdered."

"I don't know," Jimmy said. "I heard whispers, you know

from people who would be afraid to mention it. Fleming has a reputation of being a tough guy. You won't mention my name, will you?"

J.C. spread his hands on the table. "I won't mention your name if you're not bullshitting us. And, if your information turns out to be a lead, I'll even give you the tape back."

"And the copies?" Jimmy asked.

J.C. hesitated. "Copies too."

Jimmy smiled.

"If it doesn't turn out to be a lead," Wally said, "we'll keep the tapes until you get it right."

Jimmy looked scared, as if he was going to cry. "You guys promised."

"We promised to give you the tapes if you helped us," J.C. said. "If the information turns out to be helpful, you'll get the tapes. By the way, where does this Fleming guy live?"

"Somewhere; the lower West End, Motheral Avenue, I think."

Wally patted Jimmy on the back. "See? Your memory is improving. If you remember anything else, call us at this number." He handed him one of J.C.'s cards.

Wally and J.C. left Jimmy sitting motionless at the table.

#

Wally and J.C. arrived at 1498 Motheral Avenue at 9:30 am Tuesday. Ralph Fleming lived in a large split-level ranch on a double lot. From what little information they had dug up, Fleming had no apparent source of income and was suspected of dealing everything from marijuana to coke. If correct, it would be hard to get any cooperation from him; streetwise pushers have terminal lockjaw.

Wally parked in the driveway in front of a three-stall garage. They walked over an expensive terra cotta walkway to his front entrance. A familiar quiz show theme played when J.C. hit the doorbell.

Ralph Fleming's 6' 4", 240-pound frame filled the doorway. Curly black hair topped his wide, large jowled face, a face with angry eyes and scarred skin. He was dressed in blue Docker's, and a matching short-sleeved shirt.

"Yeah?" he said, looking at Wally and J.C. as if they were extraterrestrials.

"I'm Wally Gustafson and this is—"

Fleming thrust open the screen door. "Fuck you want?" he said, glaring at Wally. "You selling bibles . . . or candy?"

"No, we're not selling anything," J.C. said watching the contempt on Fleming's face grow.

"Well what then? Did some old lady lose her kitty or something?"

"No," Wally said. "I just wanted to ask you a few questions, that's all."

"Well I ain't got time for questions," Fleming said and started to close the door.

"It's about Jason Saxberg," J.C. said, trying to hold the door open.

"Who? I don't know any Saxberg. Leave me alone," Fleming said, wrenching the dor away from J.C. and slamming it.

"He's not very talkative," Wally said.

"That's true. He's not very friendly either."

Wally winked his eye. "Looks like a candidate for a surveil."

Chapter 15

Paul was in a huff as he left headquarters and headed for the Page Steel & Wire Plant to talk to Matthew's supervisor. That morning, the commander had bumped into Paul in the hall and made a sarcastic reference to Paul's handling of the Smith case. He said a week had gone by and Paul hadn't even talked to Matthew's boss.

When Paul arrived at Pages, he parked his sedan in the cramped parking lot, locked it and headed for the guard shack. He wasn't looking for anything specific; he just wanted to ask some routine questions.

The noise of his footsteps broke the silence as he walked across the glittery, sandpaper-like mill dust. After explaining the purpose of his visit to the guard, Paul was supplied with a hard-hat and safety glasses, as well as a pudgy guide named "Smokey" who would lead him to the galvanize department.

Smokey pointed to various machines while explaining the many processes of wire making. He talked like a tour guide, but as Paul's senses came alive with these new sights and sounds, Smokey's voice seemed to wane. As they walked through the wiredrawing department, the smell of the soap

104

used to facilitate the pulling of wire through a die clung to Paul's nostrils. The pungent odor of acid was overwhelming as they passed the cleaning house where the wire's surface was being purified. The rod mill department was off to the left. Red hot rods streaking like snakes wound their way around rollers and through dies that reduced their size from billets to workable sizes of wire.

As they approached the galvanize department, the noise became much louder. The constant whirling of machinery and whooshing of fire-breathing furnaces fascinated Paul. Smokey explained that the wire was being treated with heat and then coated with zinc to preserve it. When they finally reached the foreman's office, Paul turned around and stared in awe at the ancient machinery and equipment. He wondered how these men could work in this environment.

Paul followed his guide into the galvanize foreman's office.

"This here's Detective Andrews," Smokey said to a bespectacled, chubby man seated behind an old oak desk. It was cluttered with papers, tags with wire wrappings and waxed papers with sandwich crumbs on them.

"Marsh, Bob Marsh," the foreman said, extending his red-and-blue plaid arm. "Have a seat. What can I help you with?"

Marsh and Paul sat in unison; Paul on a metal folding chair.

"I'd like some information on Matthew Smith," Paul said.

"Is he in some kind of trouble?" Marsh asked as he hunched forward looking over his spectacles. He turned to Smokey and said, "Have Palmer call out Wallace, we'll probably need an extra laborer."

Smokey's footsteps kicked up a cloud of gray dust as he walked away.

Paul started to get a sick feeling in his stomach. Now that his guide was gone, he was worried about finding his own way out of the mill. He turned to the foreman. "No, just routine questions. You know his father was found dead?"

"Yeah, we had to change the schedule over that; had to pay overtime to Bucky Johnson for three days."

What a heart. "I understand he worked midnight on the eighteenth?"

Marsh bent over and opened the bottom left drawer of his desk, his bald pate shining where patent furnace dust hadn't yet reached. He grabbed a fistful of papers and plopped them on the desk. He shuffled through them until he found what he was looking for. "Yeah, he worked the first turn . . . yeah, Tuesday."

"Is that eleven to seven, or twelve to eight?"

"Twelve to seven," Marsh said, looking at the sheet. "He left an hour early, said he was sick. I docked him an hour's pay."

Paul bent forward, almost leaning on Marsh's desk. "Did he say what was wrong?"

"Nope, didn't ask either."

"What kind of employee is he? How's his work?"

"He gets by," Marsh said, then looked at Paul. "He's not too strong or too bright. He's very shy . . . doesn't think very much of himself. Gets his work done, but he won't advance around here."

"Why would you say that?" Paul asked. "I mean about him not thinking very much of himself."

"He's a negative person," Marsh said. "He runs himself down."

"In what way?"

"By the way he talks about himself . . . by his actions. I think he has an inferiority complex?"

"Can you elaborate?" Paul said, wanting a more descriptive answer. "Can you give me some examples?"

Marsh shifted in his seat, scratched his head and then opened his hands as if offering the only explanation. "When I ask him to do something, he asks a lot of questions . . . like he isn't sure of himself. The other day I asked him to take the scrap to the scrap-bailer; he said a truck was blocking the entrance, that he'd have to wait."

"What's wrong with that?"

"Nothing, if that was the only entrance to the rod mill." Marsh said. He cocked his head at Paul, then seemed to realize Paul didn't understand. "That's where the scrap-bailer is," he added.

"Does he do this all the time?"

"All the time. When I question him about it, he says he's not sure of himself, that he wants to do the right thing."

Paul looked out the foreman's window at the men working and asked, "Does Matthew drink or take drugs?"

"Not that I know of."

"Does he have a temper?"

"Yes, I've seen him get mad. Not when he notices that I'm around, but yes, I've seen him angry."

"Have you ever heard him talk about his father?"

"No. He doesn't talk to me much," Marsh said, "especially about personal matters."

"What about his friends? Does he have any close friends?"

"He talks to Timothy Magotz a lot," Marsh said, pointing out the window to a young man picking up scrap. "That's him there. Marsh had indicated a young, short man in his early twenties. He had very dark hair, but his skin looked like the belly of a catfish. "I guess that's the only friend he has here."

Paul jotted Magotz's name down in his notepad. He also realized that the missing hour from seven to eight a.m. was more important. He remembered that Matthew didn't mention leaving early in his statement. He also knew that this omission was damaging as it provided Matthew an opportunity for the murder of his father.

"Thanks a lot, Mr. Marsh," Paul said handing him his card. "If you think of anything else, please call this number."

"Sure thing."

At Paul's insistence, Marsh provided a laborer to escort him out of the mill.

#

Wally and Paul were seated in their favorite booth, the large, corner one strategically placed between the kitchen and the bar. J.C. pushed the buzzer at the service window. Nuggets appeared.

Before J.C. could give an order, Wally yelled, "I'll have '*Sex on the Beach*'."

J.C. turned around wondering if Wally really wanted that drink.

Paul winked at J.C. "Maybe you'd better make that '*brains*'; Wally could make better use of it."

J.C. picked up the tray of three I.C. Lights and a double shot of bourbon that Nuggets pushed through the service window and put them on the table. Paul threw down his shot with a backward head thrust followed by a gulp of beer. Wally and J.C. re-filled their mugs and took a sip.

"Never saw an old mill like that before," Paul said, his face contorted from the taste of the shot. "Everything was so old. All the work had to be done by hand. They were replacing acid into wire cleaning vats from large, wood-framed bottles. It took two laborers to lift a bottle. Another worker was dipping molten lead from a lead pan with a small bucket at the end of a steel bar. Can you imagine the weight of a lead-filled bucket at the end of a six-foot bar? Hell, it wasn't until five years ago that they got electric cranes to lift three-hundred-pound bundles of wire onto the reels."

"It's an old mill," Wally said. "I think it was built in nineteen oh seven."

"Yeah," Paul said, "and probably has the same equipment— except for the cranes."

J.C. changed the subject. "What did the foreman say?"

"Surprise," Paul said, leaning forward on the table. "Matthew left an hour early on the morning of the murder."

"That could turn out to be very important," Wally said. "Anything else?"

"Not much. Seems Matthew doesn't think a lot about himself though. Has a temper, doesn't talk to anyone except his only friend, a guy named Bruce Magotz. Anybody know him?'

J.C. shook his head sideways as he looked at Wally. "No," Wally said.

"Well, at least we've got one thing," Paul said. "If Matthew's one-hour absence from work can't be explained, he'll become a suspect and be brought in for questioning."

Barb came in and slid into the booth next to J.C.

He put his arm around her shoulder. "How was your day?" he said, wondering if she had time to check up on Ruth at the hospital.

"Long. Shift and a half. Get that about twice a week."

"Did you have time to—?"

"Yes I did. I talked to my friend, Linda in records. She knows everything about everybody, and if she doesn't, she looks it up."

Paul had a confused look on his face. "Is she allowed to snoop in people's records?"

"Well, not really. She's not supposed to read them, just update and file them. Only her supervisor could see what she was doing and she said he was out to lunch."

"Did she find anything?" J.C. asked.

"No."

Paul took a swig of beer and said, "That'll cut my interview with Ruth's supervisor short."

Barb looked across the table at J.C. "What about that run-in you had the other day?" Then she looked at Paul. "What did the police find out?"

"They gave the case to Pastorkovich," Paul said. "He took tire impressions at the scene today. It'll be hard to find a match. Even if he does, it'll turn out to be stolen."

"You sure it'll be stolen?" Barb asked.

"Someone who planned a crime usually wouldn't use their own car.

"You were lucky," Barb said. "You were unharmed and managed to get away from a gun-wielding crazy man without getting hurt."

"I don't think crazy is the right word," J.C. added. "It looked pretty deliberate to me. Wally and I were talking earlier. Maybe it's the same guy from three years ago. Maybe that accident I had with the brakes wasn't an accident at all."

Paul looked as if he was thinking. "Finding out who you really are will solve all the other questions. There has to be a connection somewhere."

"I hope we find it soon," J.C. said.

Chapter 16

Thursday's early morning sun shone into headquarters' parking lot as Paul drove off. He thought the logical place to investigate the reverend's alleged child abuse would be to go where he lived and worked—The United Methodist Church. But to whom would he talk? Who would recognize child abuse, especially any commmitted by the reverend? He had to find someone who knew abuse firsthand, was the same age as the reverend's children and who was in the classroom to witness it.

Paul walked into the empty basement where children's Bible study classes were held. He found communion photo albums in a bookshelf at the far end of the hall. He flipped through pages until he found a picture of a graduating class with the reverend's children in it. He scanned the childish faces, hoping to recognize one that might help him. He found the boy he was looking for. His face stuck out like a Catholic priest at a bar mitzvah. Jim Michaels was the man he wanted to see. Michaels knew all the kids in the picture and he also knew about abuse.

Paul had been on the force about ten years when he handled the Michaels' case. Michaels was about eighteen when he was arrested for almost beating his father to death. His defense was emotional abuse. The judge gave him a choice; two years in jail or two years in the army. He chose the barrack's life. After the service, he moved back to Greenville, but not with his parents. Paul stuck the communion picture under his jacket, went home and called Michaels to set up a meeting. Michaels agreed.

#

The drive to Roosevelt Street didn't take long. The Michaels' house was third from the corner, a brick bungalow with a glass-enclosed front porch that provided a haven for flowering plants.

Paul knocked on the door. Michaels walked through an interior doorway. He looked much bigger than he remembered. He was about 6'2" and 240 pounds.

"Mister Andrews," Jim said cordially. "Good to see you; come on in."

The sun porch was shaded from the afternoon sun. Jim motioned Paul toward a wicker chair.

"What can I do for you?"

"I need your help," Paul said. "I guess you've heard about Reverend Smith, haven't you?"

He nodded. "How can I help?"

"I believe he was abusive toward his family," Paul said. "I need witnesses to prove it. You know about abuse. Can you tell me if the reverend was abusive to anyone in your communion class?"

"You mean sexual abuse? Why should I?" he asked, frowning. "If he was abusive toward his family and others, he deserved to be murdered."

Paul could see the anger developing in Jim's eyes. "Nobody deserves to be murdered or sexually abused, but abusers need to be exposed, to prevent it from happening again. The more we bring this problem to the attention of the public, the more it can be dealt with."

Jim looked out the window, between a potted begonia and a miniature rose, and stared into the distance.

Paul continued. "Once you understood abuse, it was easier to deal with, wasn't it? I'm investigating a murder here. Did you see any abuse or not?"

Jim hesitated, lit a cigarette, and finally seemed resigned to the situation. "What can I do for you?"

Paul showed him the communion picture and asked him to look it over. "Is there anyone in this picture that you know was abused by Reverend Smith?"

"Well . . . his kids . . . I don't know about sexually, but he was always running them down, using them as examples."

"Any others know about this?"

Jim studied the picture, commenting on certain friends and what they were presently doing. Then he pointed to one boy, "Harrold Stuhl, yeah, the reverend constantly gave Harrold a hard time."

Paul was writing Stuhl's name on his note pad when Jim recognized another young boy, Brian Whethers.

"Are they the only ones?" Paul asked.

"Other than his own kids, yeah."

"What about these two? Why not others? Were they different?"

"They were frail kids, the kind that wouldn't talk back," Jim said. "They were sort of effeminate, you know, sissies."

"Did the other kids pick on them?"

"Not at first, but later on, after the reverend browbeat them, they started."

"You said the reverend abused his own kids, right?"

"Right, Brian and Harrold too," Jim said. "Brian and Harrold were sexually molested. I heard them talking one day."

"Can I count on you for a statement to that effect?"

"Yeah, I'll help out."

Paul thanked him and left. He knew it would be hard to prove abuse by the reverend; his actions would be made to appear as those of a strict disciplinarian. But sexual abuse was another matter. Brian and Harrold could unlock the reverend's mystery chest.

#

Wally spent an hour in his kitchen, cooking another home-cooked dinner for Paul, who usually ate out or skipped a meal in favor of alcohol. Wally had his usual chef's hat on; it looked like a vacuum sweeper bag, only white. His favorite apron was red, to match tomato sauce and not display his clumsiness. He had sewed Velcro patches on it to eliminate the loose, long ties.

"Smells good, Uncle Wally" Paul said, walking toward the stove where Wally was carefully inspecting his work. "Hmmm, halupki, I love 'em."

"These aren't halupki, my dear Watson." Wally looked defiant. "Halupki is Slovak. These are Galumbki; they're Polish."

"A stuffed cabbage roll by any other name is still a Polish hand grenade."

Wally held up a large, wooden spoon. "With the special seasoning I'm adding, it's Polish."

"Well, from what I heard, along with that special seasoning, you'd better add some *Beano*."

Wally shot a wicked glance at Paul.

"How soon 'til it's ready?"

"For you, about fifteen minutes."

Paul decided to call Councilman Ted Martinet and used the phone in Wally's living room. He knew he'd have to interview Stuhl and Whethers, but wanted corroboration also.

"Ted, Paul Andrews."

"Hi, Paul. What can I do for you?"

"When I talked to you at Reverend Smith's funeral, you seemed to be concerned about the investigation."

"Yes, yes, I am."

"I'm having a little problem that you might take care of."

"What's that?" Ted spoke as if he already knew there would be a problem. "What do you have in mind?"

"I need some information on the reverend's background. Can you dig something up for me?

"Absolutely," Ted said, sounding more enthusiastic. "I've already started. Is there anything in particular you're looking for?"

"A motive, anything that might be helpful in my investigation."

"What kind of motive. Anything special?"

"The sexual abuse theory you mentioned might be a starting point."

"I've been asking around, but nothing yet. I have a few people to talk to, though."

"I appreciate it,"

Paul knew that Martinet could pry information from a deaf mute. He was a politician, a good one. He knew how to work the system, where to go, who to talk to. If anyone could go back in time and retrieve sensitive information, Martinet was the one to do it.

#

J.C. wiped spilled beer from the bar—the result of an argument between George "Moldy" Rixey and James "Tex" Yates. The two avid fishermen had just come back from a day's angling at Dutch Fork Lake.

Moldy had opened his creel and proudly displayed his catch of three trout and one bass to Nuggets and the patrons at the bar. When Tex opened his creel, he pulled out a box of Mrs. Filbert's Fish Sticks that Moldy had secretly placed there. Tex's field goal attempt with the box of fish sticks went wide and knocked over a glass of Bud Light in front of a patron who had to jump up to keep the beer from spilling into his lap.

Moldy brought in Tex's real catch as the phone rang.

"Ducheck's," J.C. answered.

"Yeah, this is Fleming. You gave me your card the other day. Remember?"

J.C. paused a moment. He was surprised at the call. "Yeah . . . Fleming, Ralph Fleming. I remember."

"I might be able to help you out. You know, what we talked about the other day."

"Good. What can you tell me?"

"Not on the phone. I'll talk to you in person."

"Okay, where can I meet you?"

"Ross Park, Pavilion Number Twelve. Tomorrow. Two-thirty. Alone. Got that?"

"Got it."

J.C. hung up, feeling energized. He felt that Fleming was the key to finding Jason's murderer. He couldn't wait to tell Wally.

Chapter 17

Paul awoke with a brutal hangover; he had drunk himself to sleep thinking about what Jim Michaels had told him about sexual abuse and the possible connection to Reverend Smith. He had scheduled time this morning to talk to Harrold Stuhl and Brian Whethers, two of the reverend's former students.

Harrold Stuhl lived above a tailor shop in the southwest part of town, formally the industrial center of the three-county area. Ruppert's Steel Mill was nearby, the largest mill in town. In its heyday, Ruppert's worked around the clock, seven days a week. People from surrounding towns would come at night to watch an aerial view of the light shows from Zayzak's hill on the other side of the river. Blast furnaces would erupt with brilliant light, spouting forth an avalanche of sparks and belching smoke with each pour of newly created steel. Pulsating red and orange glows of light streamed from the hot billets as they wound their way through various reducing stages until flat steel or rods were produced.

The mill seemed alive, an iron-and-steel, fire-breathing animal with hundreds of men working in its entrails. They fed it large amounts of crude materials from railway cars. They had to keep the monster alive; it kept the city alive.

Paul drove past Ruppert's, one of three mills in Greenville, turned left on Alliquippa Avenue and headed toward 35ᵗʰ St. All the mills were vacant now. The mass exodus of workers had left businesses, like Skarzenski's corner deli, near bankruptcy. At one time, there were twelve hotels in this part of town and thirty-one bars. The hotels were gone; twenty bars remained.

Paul checked the two mailboxes at the entrance next to the tailor shop and walked up the splintered, creaky steps to the second floor. Harrold Stuhl's apartment was at the end of the dark, narrow hallway. The walls were stained and disfigured by years of neglect. One broken light bulb hung from an extension cord.

Paul knocked on the door. As he prepared to knock again, the door cracked open. The first thing Paul noticed about Harrold was a pair of sad, old eyes on a thin, ashen face that looked older than the late thirties Paul knew him to be. He was about five' five", 140 pounds and had long dyed black hair. He was wearing a blue terry cloth robe and green furry slippers.

Paul introduced himself. Harrold invited him in. The apartment was retro forties; doilies on the old couches and chairs, flower print carpeting and an old tube-type radio. The fireplace mantel that hung over its ceramic firebox displayed old family photos. One was a recent photo of a young man. It looked as if it had been crumpled and smoothed out again, then pressed back into its cracked glass frame.

"What can I help you with?" Harrold asked. "Is it about the rent money?"

"No, I'm trying to get some information about Reverend Smith. Did you hear he was murdered?"

"Yes, I heard," he said nonchalantly.

"Do you know of anyone who would want to harm the reverend?"

"Yes, a few people," he said, "including me. Is that why you're here?"

"What can you tell me about him?"

"He didn't like me; he treated me like shit. He was a reverend in title only. He wasn't a Christian, that's for sure."

"Why would you say that?" Paul asked, scanning the room again for potential clues.

"He knew I was different. He didn't discourage the others from making fun of me. He lectured me in front of the class about the word of God."

"What do you mean . . . different?" Paul asked. He knew the answer.

"I'm gay. The reverend couldn't get past that." Harrold's voice cracked as he spoke louder. "He'd lecture me, ridicule me and have the others do it too."

"Would you term his behavior toward you as abusive?"

"Classical."

"Did the reverend abuse anyone else in the class?"

"Other than his kids, yeah, Brian Whethers," Harrold said, his voice lowering in pitch and intensity. "He treated him like shit too."

"Was it the same reason as you?"

"Yeah, same reason."

"Where do you work . . . in case I have to reach you?"

"Eisenberg's Dress Shop. I'm off today."

"What do you do there?"

"I'm a salesperson and window dresser," he said, tilting his head in an upward, proud manner.

"One other thing. Did the reverend's abuse go beyond what you told me?"

"You mean did he sexually abuse me also?" He asked, nervously pacing around. "Yes. He said it was punishment for not obeying God's word."

Paul was surprised at his candidness. "Were there any others?"

"Not that I'm aware of," Harrold said.

Twenty-five minutes later, Paul was across town at Brian Whethers' driveway. He lived in a Mediterranean ranch on a large lot in an affluent neighborhood, the polar opposite of Harrold Stuhl's squalid flat. Brian was cleaning his golf clubs at the front of his three-stall garage as Paul approached him.

Tall, handsome and muscular, Brian looked fifteen years younger than Harold, although the two men were the same age. He corroborated Harrold's assessment of the reverend in every detail. He said that in addition to the reverend's children he was the brunt of the reverend's abuse also, but not the sexual side of it.

Paul thought the reverend might have picked on the weak, frail boys, to show his superiority, but as he looked at Brian he discounted that theory. The common denominator, although one was sexually abused, was that both were gay. Paul theorized that outside of his own family, which he apparently abused often, the reverend probably targeted gays, sometimes sexually. This was something he would have to investigate further.

#

The phone rang at two-thirty. Paul hated calls at this time; he allocated the last hour-and-a-half of his day for paperwork and research.

"Detective Andrews?" It was a man's voice.

"Yes. This is Detective Andrews. How can I help you?"

"I called to help you." The voice changed to a sexy, boudoir tone. "But maybe you can help me later?"

"Who is this?"

"It's Leslie . . . Leslie Carter. Have you forgotten me so soon?"

Paul searched his memory banks for a man named Leslie. There must have been a withdrawal. No Leslie Carter. "I'm sorry, I—"

"Leslie Carter. I met you at the Velvet Slipper. Don't you remember?"

Paul's face took on a pink glow; he slumped back in his chair. *It's the transvestite. What the hell's she—er—he doing calling me here?* Then he remembered giving her/him his card.

"Yes, now I remember. What kind of help? Do you have any information for me?"

"You might want to talk to Ralph Fleming."

"Who's that?"

"He's a pusher. Word is he sold to Jason and his boyfriend."

Paul perked up. A boyfriend! This could be the lead he was looking for. "Who's his boyfriend?"

"Don't know. People are afraid to talk."

"Why?"

"Fleming's connected. I hear he sells to some very influential people. I'm nervous myself. That's all I can tell you. Don't mention my name, okay?"

"I won't. Anything else?"

"Well . . . you could show your gratitude. Buy me a drink sometime?"

"Maybe tear up a parking ticket or float a free pass on a misdemeanor," Paul said, feeling both grateful for the tip and annoyed at the proposition. "I'm on the men's team and I don't switch sides. Don't forget it, okay."

Leslie hung up with a pouting, "Okay."

Chapter 18

The suburbs started to disappear as J.C. headed toward Ross Park. He was early for his 2:00 p.m. meeting with Fleming and passed the time thinking of Barb and how he wanted her in his life. He knew he could only have her with his past cleared up, that is, if it was a reputable past. He wouldn't settle for anything less; he wouldn't take a chance on hurting her.

He drove a "98" Oldsmobile, a loaner car, provided by the garage while his Bronco was being repaired. Fleming had been hostile toward him at his home, but when J.C. talked to him on the phone, he sounded like he wanted to help. He thought that Fleming's sudden change of attitude might shed some light on the case.

J.C. drove along the peaceful, tree-lined road that wound its way through the park. The near-perfect weather and the gorgeous landscape calmed him to the extent that he wanted to forget about his problems, including the fact that someone was trying to kill him. But his mind wouldn't let go. Could it be Fleming? Why would he want to meet at this remote location? It could be an ambush. Maybe he was the one in the dark truck. He hadn't seen anyone in the park; it was desolate and gave him an uneasy feeling he hadn't had for a while. It's a good thing, he thought, that Wally was already in the park, making his way through the woods toward Pavilion Number Twelve, as they had planned.

#

Wally parked his Chevy two pavilions away at Number Ten, far enough away as not to be seen, but close enough to reach J.C. quickly if he needed help. He unlocked the equipment case in the bed of the truck and grabbed his binoculars. His Taurus 9mm was tucked under a blanket with a six-pack of ammo magazines. He grabbed one and shoved it into the auto's handle. He stored three more in his pockets. He traded his gold, cotton jacket for one of the cammo shirts he had bought at the Army Navy Store. Wally also brought along two large plastic wire tie-wraps, the kind electricians use, in lieu of handcuffs. He had seen police use them on "Cops, Cops."

The trees at the bend of the road obscured Wally's vision of Pavilion Number Elevenonly a block away. The road made another bend farther up, about the same distance, to where Pavilion Number Twelve would be. Between the road and a small creek that ran parallel to it, an open space of sixty yards was cleared for picnickers. On the other side of the stream, a dense cover of young pines and laurel bushes blended into the surrounding county forest.

A number of flat rocks rose above the water level, providing Wally easy access to the other side. Although the wooded area was dense, walking was easy. The pines dropped enough needles to furnish a thick mulch, keeping weeds and shrubs to a minimum.

Wally quickly walked to Pavilion Number Eleven, but realized the rest of the way would be a lot harder. The pines became sparse and gave way to thorny nuisance bushes,

poison ivy, scrub trees, fallen dead branches, and toppled
tree trunks. The remaining taller trees were part of a thick
hardwood forest. The dense underbrush slowed walking
considerably as did the need for silence. Suddenly, the
terrain became hilly. Wally stopped at a large red maple on
top of a knoll. He scanned the area in the direction of Pavilion
Number Twelve with his binoculars. He didn't see anyone
other than Fleming. His Cadillac was the only vehicle in the
parking lot. Maples are good climbing trees; they have low,
parallel branches that provide easy access to other branches.
Wally scraped his forearms and wrists climbing the tree for a
better look. J.C. hadn't arrived yet. Wally climbed higher
and scanned the area again. He took his time; it was the last
available high spot before reaching the pavilion.

#

J.C. drove into the lot and parked next to Fleming's
Caddy. He got out, looked around cautiously and headed
for the pavilion. He didn't know what to expect and was
very nervous. Fleming had a bad reputation and had
suddenly changed his mind about this meeting, giving J.C.
pause.

Fleming sat on top of a wooden picnic table, near the
fireplace. J.C. walked in and sat on an adjoining table,
keeping Fleming between him and the woods.

#

Wally had checked most of the area and it looked okay.
He was about ready to climb down when a glint of light
caught his attention. It quickly disappeared and reappeared
again in the creek-bed about fifty yards from the pavilion.
He focused on the area with his binoculars and spotted a
man kneeling in the creek-bed, next to the bank behind a

tree, his head sticking just above ground level. The reflection he saw probably came from the metallic frame of the man's sunglasses.

The area between Wally and this back-up man—or paid assassin—was a gently sloping wooded stretch of approximately 200 yards. Wally had to circle around another hilly knoll to avoid detection. He wondered if he would make it in time for the meeting; he had ten minutes. Although the dense area and the hill obstructed his movement, he made progress. He came to a small valley directly behind the man, allowing him silent, unseen access. The grass sod muffled Wally's footsteps. In moments, thirty yards separated him from the gunman. He stopped behind a tree and carefully checked out the area. He listened for the slightest noise and, from his position, could watch Fleming and the man in the creek-bed at the same time. He waited to see or hear if anything or anyone else was in the area.

Silence covered the area like a blanket. Wally waited for J.C. to appear before making his move. Five minutes went by before J.C. drove up. Wally watched the two men as J.C. approached. He drew his 9mm and carefully crept up on the man in the creek. The man looked young, about twenty-five with long brown hair. He wore blue coveralls and a red plaid shirt. The reflection from the metallic frames on his tan sunglasses had given away his position. Wally saw that both of the man's hands were empty. Keeping an eye on Fleming, Wally approached, creeping up behind the gunman.

Wally crept within five yards of the man. He didn't want to startle Fleming so he whispered, "Don't move, keep your hands in sight and don't say anything."

The man looked surprised. He froze.

"Put your hands behind you," Wally said reaching for a plastic tie-wrap. He deftly looped it over the man's wrists and tightened it with a yank. Wally stood him up and patted him down for weapons. He was clean.

"What's your name?" Wally whispered. "and keep your voice down."

"Ben Hawkins." Wally saw a smirk appear on his face.

Wally grabbed the man's wallet and checked his ID.

"Okay Hawkins, stand up." Wally grabbed Hawkins' arm as he teetered to his feet. Wally walked him toward the pavilion.

"What the hell—" Fleming said as the two men approached.

J.C's mouth fell open as he tried to stand up, but he dropped to the seat again.

"I didn't know you needed an audience to talk to J.C.," Wally said to Fleming. "We could've met on the street."

Fleming glared at Hawkins differently than he would have had he made a mistake, more like he was studying his face. "Just covering my ass, that's all."

"Stand up," Wally said to Fleming, and then patted him down. "Just covering *my* ass that's all."

J.C. pointed a finger at Fleming. "What the hell is this? Were you thinking of doing something stupid?"

Fleming leered at Hawkins with a look of disgust. He didn't answer.

By the look on Hawkins' face, Wally could tell that Hawkins feared Fleming. Was it because Wally caught him or that he wasn't supposed to be there? Fleming seemed surprised to see Hawkins, then covered up for him. That might have been the reason that Hawkins got scared— Fleming would want to know that information. But who sent Hawkins? And why? J.C. separated the two until he found out what he came for. He'd worry about the rest later.

J.C. took Fleming to the back of the pavilion, to the rear of the barbeque. "Now, let's get down to business. What do you want to tell me?"

Fleming glared at him. "First of all, who told you to talk to me?"

"I can't answer that. It's confidential, just like our conversation."

"Okay," Fleming said, as if he knew who it was anyway. "You want to know about Saxberg, don't you?" he asked.

"That's right."

"He had a boyfriend, not just any boyfriend, but a secret boyfriend."

"Why did he want to keep him secret?"

"Saxberg didn't want to keep him a secret, the boyfriend wanted to keep it a secret," Fleming said, showing his annoyance. "He didn't want to come out of the closet."

"Okay, that's his problem. Who is he?"

"I don't know, but you can find out through his girlfriend," he said.

"A girlfriend?"

"Yeah, she's a lesbian who's also in the closet. It's one of those mutually agreed on things. You know, to keep their parents from finding out."

"Who is she?" J.C. asked.

"I don't know," he said. "Saxberg wouldn't name any names. All he said was that she was a pretty redhead."

"How did you know Saxberg?" J.C. asked.

Fleming looked at J.C. and grinned. "Let's just say it was business and leave it at that."

J.C. knew by Fleming's tone of voice that he wasn't going to volunteer any more information. He got what he came for. "Okay, thanks. You can go now and take your friend with you."

"I think I'll let him walk," Fleming said, moving toward his Cadillac.

Wally snipped the wire-tie on Hawkins' wrists. Fleming drove off. Hawkins walked in the opposite direction and disappeared behind the trees.

"Did you notice anything peculiar about Fleming's reaction toward Hawkins?" J.C. asked.

"Yeah, he seemed surprised to see him."

J.C. stroked his chin. "Wonder what that's all about?"

"What did Fleming tell you?"

J.C. recounted Fleming's story. "Looks like we have to find the pretty redhead. I wonder where we can start?"

"How about Fine's Funeral Home?" Wally said.

Chapter 19

Similar to other city parks in Greenville, Shuster's Park
provided recreation and solace for families escaping the
drudgeries of daily boredom—except for today. A body was
discovered near Pavilion Number Four in an industrial-sized
black plastic garbage bag. A jogger found the insect-infested,
rumpled bag at 7:30 a.m. on the side of a road in the picnic
area. He had noticed human fingers protruding from a torn
area of the bag and called the police.

The park bordered state game lands in an isolated area
of the city's northern tier. Roads from four entrances lead
through the park, past ball fields and playgrounds, to a lake
at the park's northernmost tip. The road where the body
was found ran along the shoreline providing access to the
eight evenly spaced picnic pavilions.

Uniformed police had already taped off the area.
Detective Paul Andrews arrived fifteen minutes later at 8:30
a.m.

Paul placed his shield on his breast pocket as he approached
a cop holding a roll of tape. "What's up officer? Whada'ya' got
here?"

"Someone threw this guy out with the garbage. Big fucker. Look at the size of his fingers."

The cop had protected the crime scene, including taping off the grassy area around the body from nosey onlookers, reporters, and even cops that might wander too close. The garbage bag was not to be opened or even touched until the crime scene guys got there.

Paul scanned the area. The body lay near a stand of evergreens on a bend in the road fifty yards from Pavilion Number Four, a rustic stone-and-log structure with a weathered, cedar-shingled roof. Grass near the berm of the blacktop had been disturbed; a small clump of sod was partially dislodged.

Paul pointed to the area. "Anyone walk through here?"

"No. I noticed that also," The cop said. "I asked the jogger how he came upon the body. He said he didn't step off the road; he didn't want to go any closer."

Paul nodded. "Anyone canvassing the area?"

"I've got two guys checking houses near the entrances, but it'll be hard. Teenagers use the park as a lover's lane. They're in and out of here most of the night. Can't pinpoint time of death until the M.E. has a look."

"Good job, officer," Paul said as forensics' white mini-van pulled up. An ambulance was close behind.

Without stopping to talk or ask questions, a forensics technician quickly donned his rubber gloves and methodically scoured the grassy area looking for footprints or any foreign material or substance and bagging cigarette butts, pop cans or anything that didn't belong in the area.

After he was satisfied that the area was clear, he cut the plastic bag away revealing a large man tied up in a fetal position. He wore a black, muscle man T-shirt, blue jeans and walking shoes. The bag was then packaged and labeled for the lab.

Paul walked over to the body where he could get a better view. The tech took pictures of the scene. A couple of onlookers gasped as the technician turned the body revealing the corpse's face. It was a grotesque sight. His eyes looked like bloodshot poached eggs with foggy, glassed-over dark yokes in the center. A black tongue hung out of the side of his exaggerated open mouth—a possible sign of strangulation.

The vicyim was a big man with raven black curly hair and scars around his eyes and cheekbones. His face had small bloody cuts on black-and-blue welts—evidence of a recent beating.

The tech pointed to the corpse's neck. "There's ligature marks on his neck."

"I see that," Paul shifted his gaze to the victim's tied hands. "There's marks around his wrists also, and not from the rope he was tied up with.

The tech looked at the marks as if he had seen them before. "Looks like handcuff marks. He was murdered and tied up later."

Paul took a closer look. He nodded in approval.

"Any identification?"

The tech dug the wallet out of the man's back pocket and dusted it for prints. He taped what he found and put the tapes in an envelope and labeled it.

He pulled some cards out of the wallet and compared a driver's license photo ID with the body. "Ralph Fleming, fourteen ninety-eight Motheral Avenue."

#

J.C. and Wally were refereeing an arm-wrestling match between two gorillas when Paul came in after work. J.C. looked relieved, knowing that any diversion, even Paul talking about a domestic dispute, would be better than watching the umteenth replay of the same weekly contest. Nuggets was tending bar, rooting the contestants on. Wally picked up his drink and headed for the back room.

"Nuggets, give Paul a drink," J.C. said as he walked to the back.

Wally and J.C. settled in their favorite booth and were soon joined by Paul with his frosty mug of I.C. Light and a double shot of Bellows.

Wally watched as Paul lumbered back to the booth. "Looks like you had a hard day Paul."

"Murders require a lot of shit paperwork—in triplicate, no less." Paul sat down and drained the shot, then took a large draw on his beer. "Fuckin' murderers don't have any consideration."

Wally looked at J.C. "We didn't hear of any murder. Where?"

"Shuster's Park," Paul said, waving his glass in that direction. "Early this morning. Someone threw a guy out with the garbage. Just like Gerri did with me only he was handcuffed and tortured.

"Whoa," Wally put his glass down. "What happened?"

"She ended it. Said she had enough of my erratic behavior."

"Sorry to hear that." J.C. said.

"It was bound to happen. We're from different planets."

Wally glanced at the empty shot-glass. "But from the same galaxy. You two were hitting it off before you took up with Mister Bellows."

J.C. saw rage starting to develop in Paul and thought he'd change the subject. "What about this guy in the park?"

Paul had to think for a moment about where he'd left off. "Some sick-ass strangled him. He was murdered elsewhere and dumped in the park."

"How do you know that?" J.C. asked.

"Because the nasty bastard re-tied the corpse with rope. Handcuff marks were on his wrists, not in the same location as the ropes. Plus the ropes didn't leave any marks which means the man was already dead."

"Who found him?" Wally asked.

"A jogger. Poor guy goes out for a morning health run,

maybe to lower his blood pressure and finds a corpse. Saw fingers pokin' out of the garbage bag."

"Who was it?" J.C. asked, and then sipped on his beer.

"Ralph Fleming," Paul slammed his mug on the table. "Lived over on Motheral Avenue. I got a tip on this guy yesterday. Didn't have a chance to talk to him," Paul made a noise like a half-chuckle, a sound of disgust. "Something else for the commander to get in my shit about." He didn't smile, but continued, "Anyway, seems he sold drugs to Jason Saxberg and might have known who his boyfriend was."

Wally and J.C. exchanged embarrassed glances. J.C. took a gulp of beer and tried to act nonchalant.

"That's too bad," Wally said, then took a large gulp of beer also.

Paul started to slide out of the booth. He started to stand, then sat down again. "By the way, one of the officers canvassing the area talked to a man who saw a dark green truck in the area. Could the truck that ran you off the road have been dark green?"

J.C. closed his eyes, trying to remember what happened that night coming home from the community college. "Could have been. It was dark. That's all I can remember."

"Okay, just a hunch." Paul drained his mug, put it on the table, and left.

"Holy shit," Wally said. "We just talked to him and now he's dead. Murdered."

J.C. leaned back against the smooth leather of the booth. "First he won't talk to us at all, then he can't wait to volunteer information. Don't you find that strange?"

"Yeah, Maybe the redhead killed him—whoever she is."

"No, I don't think so. A woman couldn't handle a body as big as Fleming," J.C. said, extending his arms to demonstrate the man's size. "Either it was Jason's murderer or someone who didn't want us to find the redhead. Maybe it's the same person."

Wally perked up. "Maybe it was that Ben Hawkins guy we found the other day in the park. Fleming knew about the redhead, Hawkins probably does, too. She may be the key that helps us find who killed Jason Saxberg."

"We'll have to talk to him," J.C. said. "I think you're right, Wally. Fleming looked surprised when he saw Hawkins. He must've been there on his own. Let's go see Hawkins now, before the police find a connection between them."

Wally hesitated. "How about I come back here in an hour? That'll give me time to grab a bite and look up Hawkins' address."

"Yeah, okay. I should change clothes anyway," J.C. said, tugging at his shirt. "I could use a bite too. By the way, don't mention Fleming's murder to Barb. I don't want her to worry."

J.C. was pacing on the sidewalk outside Ducheck's when Wally drove up. Before the truck had stopped, J.C. yanked the door open and jumped in the cab. "Did you get his address?"

"Sure did." Wally answered. "Eight twenty-four Luce Avenue. West Side."

"Is that near Sacred Heart Hospital?"

"A little south of the hospital," Wally said. "Toward the bend in the river."

"That's near the 'Sit n Bull', isn't it?"

Wally eyes widened looking at J.C. "Yeah, come to think of it."

"Coincidence?" J.C. asked as Wally turned onto Luce Avenue.

A 1998 black Bravada sat in Hawkins' driveway, facing the street. As they pulled up Hawkins peered from around the back of the S.U.V. He was under lift gate and quickly closed it.

Wally pulled into the driveway. "Let's find out."

Hawkins jutted his head around the side of the vehicle like a chipmunk looking for a nut. He slammed the lift gate shut, walked forward, and stood near the front bumper.

An old garage with crooked barn-type doors and windows with missing panes stood at the end of the driveway, about twenty yards from the house. Peeling white paint gave the exterior a feathery look, exposing a dark gray under-painting. The two-storey house resembled the garage.

"What d'ya' want?" Hawkins said, shuffling his feet and folding and unfolding his arms. "Can you come back? I'm kinda' busy."

"We just want to ask you a few questions," J.C. said, walking toward Hawkins.

Hawkins took a step back. "About what?"

"About a redhead," Wally said. "We want to know who she is and where to find her."

Hawkins jammed his hands into his pockets. "A redhead? I don't know any redhead."

"Fleming said you did," J.C. said.

Hawkins jerked his head in J.C.'s direction, eyes wide. He looked down. His lip seemed to tremble. His head darted around. He seemed to be looking for an answer.

"We have time," Wally said. "We can wait all day if you want, but we won't leave without that name."

J.C. interrupted with a wild guess. "I think the police would like to know about the connection between you and Fleming. Did you know the cops found his body early this morning—in a garbage bag?"

Hawkins seemed nervous, as if he had to make a quick exit. He turned slowly to his right, faking a look at the right passenger tire on his vehicle. That's when he threw a roundhouse right. J.C. instinctively leaned to his left, parried the blow with his right arm and, at the same time, wrapped his arm around Hawkins' arm, bending it behind him. As he performed this lightning-fast feat with his right arm, he reached around Hawkins' throat with his left arm and grabbed his right shoulder sleeve.

J.C. applied pressure to Hawkins' arm and throat. "Now what were you going to tell me?"

Hawkins sputtered. "I don't know. Fleming—"

"Wrong answer," J.C. applied more pressure. "I heard twenty pounds of pressure will break an arm. Want to go for it?"

"I told you, I don't know—"

J.C. lifted Hawkins off the ground, whose face was turning crimson.

"Don't kill him," Wally said. "We'll never get an answer that way."

J.C. eased up the pressure on Hawkins' throat and arm.

After a few moments, Hawkins caught his breath; his eyes squinted and narrowed in pain. "Okay, okay, you sick fuck. Ka . . . Katie. Katie's her name. Katie McClure. All right?"

"That's a nice name," J.C. said torquing up the pressure. "Now where does she live?"

Hawkins grumbled something under his breath. When J.C. applied more pressure, Hawkins barked out, "Madison. She lives in Madison."

"All right," Wally said in a consoling tone. "Now that was easy, wasn't it?"

Chapter 20

Paul called Matthew Smith at 8:30 a.m. He thought Matthew would be at home since he had worked yesterday's 4X12 shift. Paul thought if he could pressure the guy a little, he could squeeze some information out of him—maybe a confession. Matthew took the call and said he could be at headquarters in an hour.

Paul had talked to Timothy Magotz the night before on information supplied by Matthew's foreman, Bob Marsh. Marsh said that Matthew and Magotz were friends, but didn't know exactly how close they were. They were close all right. Magotz revealed that Matthew hated his father, that he wished he were dead. Paul called Captain Henderson at home and reported his findings and said that he was going to call Matthew in.

Paul told the desk sergeant to have someone bring Matthew to the second floor interrogation room, or sweat room as he called it, when he arrived. He asked Pastorkovich—everyone calls him Pastor—to join him in the interrogation. Paul didn't have much time to fill him in on what he was going to do. He just wanted Pastor to sit there and look mean; Pastor was very good at that. The captain and another detective would be in a small, adjacent room observing through a one-way mirror. They could also hear them from microphones that were placed throughout the room.

The desk sergeant buzzed Paul and said an officer was bringing Matthew to the sweat room. Paul looked out the door and watched Matthew as he followed the officer down the hall. Matthew looked as if he was being led to the gallows.

"Hi Matt," Paul said, starting off in a disarmingly pleasant mood. "Right this way." Paul motioned with his arm toward the door. Matthew mumbled some kind of greeting.

"Thanks for coming. This shouldn't take long," Paul said, opening the door. Paul motioned for Matthew to sit in the chair opposite the one-way mirror so the observers in the viewing room could watch his face. Paul took the chair opposite. Pastor manhandled the door as he came in the room. Matthew looked up, at Pastor's six-four frame, slid his hands in his pockets, and looked away. Pastor sat to Paul's left, his large frame blocking physically and psychologically, any means of Matthew's escape.

After Paul read Matthew his rights, and informed him again about retaining counsel, Matthew agreed to being questioned and signed a release form.

"I just want to ask you a few questions to clear up a few things," Paul said in a reassuring tone. "Okay?"

"Yeah, sure," Matthew said as he lowered his head and rubbed his finger over an imaginary smudge on the tabletop.

After starting the tape recorder and having Matthew repeat his name and address, Paul began the questioning. "You work at Page's don't you?"

"Yes."

"What's your job there, Matthew?"

"I'm a reeler. A reeler on number one patent furnace."

"What's a reeler do?"

"I load the bundles of wire on reels," Matthew said,

moving his finger in a circular pattern. "They turn around as the wire's being pulled through the furnace. When that bundle's running, I load another on the top part of the reel."

"Sounds like hard work."

"You bet, some of those bundles are four hundred pounds." Matthew sounded defensive.

"No shit! How do you manage to load them?"

"We use these small electric hand cranes now, but we used to load them by hand," Matthew said proudly, smiling, now all full of himself as if he had actually accomplished something that would alter humanity.

"How could you lift four hundred pounds?"

"It does take a knack, but you have to be strong, too."

"I guess you wouldn't have any trouble picking up a two hundred and thirty pound body then, would you?" Paul said, looking Matthew right in the eye. Paul watched te young man closely for his reaction, hoping he would say something that would soon close the case.

Matthew looked at Paul as if he was disappointed. "I don't know. What do you mean?"

"Someone had to pick up your father to clean him up, change his clothing, and the bed linens. It was you, wasn't it?"

"No, I didn't—"

"I talked to your foreman," Paul said, raising his voice, pushing the envelope. "You left work early that morning—"

"I was—"

"You told him you were sick. You lied didn't you?" Paul said, standing up, bending over Matthew, relentless. "You killed your father, didn't you? You hated him, didn't you?"

"No, no, no . . ." Matthew said, burying his face in his hands. "He was dead when I got there; he was already dead." He started to sob.

"Why did you lie? Why did you say you were sick?"

"I had to," Matthew said, between sobs. "I couldn't tell Marsh I was going fishing; he'd get pissed."

"Fishing? What the hell were you doing in your parent's house if you were going fishing?"

"I went to get my rods and tackle box," Matthew said, looking at Paul's puzzled face. "My apartment is small and I don't have a lot of storage. I keep a lot of my stuff at the parsonage."

"So you left work early to go fishing," Paul said, slowly walking around the room, looking at the ceiling, waving his arms in disbelief. "Then you went to your parents' house to get your fishing shit. Right?"

"That's right."

"Do you expect me to believe that?" Paul said. "Do you believe that detective Pastorkovich?"

"Not a fucking, single word of it," Pastor said, glaring at Matthew. "He must take us for fools."

"No, no it's true. Check out the basement. My gear's ready to go," Matthew babbled.

"You could've gotten it together after everyone left," Paul said. "Why should we believe you? You lied to us already."

"Why would I want to kill my father? I didn't have any reason to—"

"Didn't you publicly say that you hated your father?"

"No. Why would—"

"Didn't you tell Timmy Magotz you hated your father and you wished him dead?"

"That was just talk, that's all," Matthew said. He looked surprised as if he had just figured out that the police really do their jobs. "You know, just a figure of speech. I didn't really mean it. Why would I want to—"

"Because your father abused you, that's why," Paul bent over to get closer to the man's face, to watch his expression. "He abused you as a child, your brother and sister too, didn't he?"

Matthew was shaking his head from side to side as if the words were finally piercing his consciousness. Paul thought Matthew was starting to break.

After another grueling half-hour of interrogation, Pastor left the room. He came back with a sandwich and a soft drink, placed it on the table and started to eat, a psychological trick to let a witness know that the police have all the time in the world.

"We know you were abused, admit it," Paul said. "Your father knew everything, didn't he? He knew what was good for you, who you talked to, what you said, didn't he?" Paul increased the speed and volume of his voice as he spoke. "You could never measure up, could you? You didn't know scripture, you weren't pure, and you were soiled, weren't you? They didn't love you because—"

"Yes, yes, stop it, stop it," Matthew screamed. Tears ran down his face. "He was a son of a bitch, I hated him, we all hated him, but I didn't kill him. I didn't kill him." His head fell onto his hands and he wept openly.

This is the perfect time for the right question, Paul thought. "Would you be willing to take a polygraph test?" He waited for Matthew's reaction. If he hesitated, he was probably lying.

"Yes, yes, I'll take any kind of test you want to give me," Matthew said, looking at Paul.

Paul felt he had all the information he could get from Matthew. He looked at Pastor who nodded in agreement.

Paul stood up and pushed his chair under the table. "We'll check out your story, Matthew. You're out of here. Don't leave town; we'll be in touch."

Chapter 21

"That's the creek, isn't it?" J.C. asked.

Early Monday morning, Wally and J.C. started driving toward Madison, a small, rural town about forty miles west of Greenville. They had just left Old Route 5 and were approaching the bridge at Cross Creek.

Wally looked left. "Yeah, six miles down that creek is where we found Jason. In the 'Sit n' Bull's parking lot." He glanced at the road ahead, and then at J.C. "I hope we find this redhead and she has information that leads to finding his murderer."

"I hope so. The cops haven't come up with anything yet," J.C. said, looking out the window at the creek, his vision interrupted as the rusty bridge girders passed his gaze.

Wally turned the radio on and pressed the button for his favorite "oldies" station. "My Boyfriend's Back" by The Angels pulsated from the speakers at 120 decibels, the threshold of pain.

"That reminds me," Wally said. "Who do you think the secret boyfriend is? I don't have a clue."

"Well . . ." J.C. hesitated, stroking his beard as if he didn't want to reveal his theory. Then he continued: "If Matthew did kill his father, he must have had a reason. Maybe that reason involved Jason Saxberg."

Wally looked as though he shared the same thought.

The only sound in the cab of the Chevy for the next fifteen minutes was the wave of oldies chasing the dust out of Wally's dashboard speakers. Wally turned the radio off when they reached Madison.

At the town's center was a small, circular park. The main road ran around the park's eighty-yard circumference, but the town's streets radiated out from it. From the air, it would resemble a giant wagon wheel. A gazebo, perched on a platform four steps high, was at its center. The whole structure looked like a picture from the past with its white painted columns and latticework that could have provided a backdrop for an old time brass band. Stately shrubs and brightly colored flowers and perennials bordered the perimeter, providing a buffer zone for the road.

A drugstore, candy shop, photography studio, bowling alley, furniture store, and a police station with a basement library surrounded the park. The storefronts would have looked right at home in a 1930's edition of *The Saturday Evening Post*. The candy store had an old-style telephone, complete with booth, where Wally found four listings for McClure in a tattered old phone book. No one in the candy store knew Katie.

Pop, at the mom and pop drugstore, knew Katie from Wally's description and scribbled a small map on the back of an old medicine label. It described in detail how to make a left at the fork of the road at the willow tree, not the oak tree. Pop went over it so many times that J.C. thought he could drive there with his eyes closed.

They drove three miles from town and found the old, weathered farmhouse in a level area of predominately rolling hills. Probably a neat, pretty little farm in its day, it now looked like a depression-era, mid-west homestead on its last legs. A

Mail Pouch Tobacco ad seemed to be holding one side of the barn together, a patch over the missing and twisted boards. The silo next to it wouldn't do the barn any favors if it fell away from it—and it looked ready to go. The squawking chickens in the yard seemed to be on strike against unfair living conditions as they bustled around, heads bobbing up and down like chipmunks on caffeine, looking as if they were waiting for the coop to keel over in a stinking heap. Even the small pond by the cattle yard had green scum on it, the color of velvet on a pool table.

Wally pulled into the driveway and parked near the remnants of what appeared to be a '56 Ford truck. He and J.C. had to walk carefully toward the house, skirting old washing machines, radios, TVs, and other assorted household items serving the dual purpose of obstacle course and ground cover for the front yard.

As they approached the porch, the front door creaked open. A tall man in bib overhauls appeared first, followed by a short, frail woman in a blue, sagging warm-up suit. The man held a walking stick in front of him and together, the couple looked like Grant Wood's *American Gothic*, except that this man had a full head of hair and the gaunt woman in Wood's picture looked healthy by comparison to the woman in blue.

"We don't want nothin', you best be on your way," the man said, the ruts in his face deepening. "This here's private property."

"We're not selling anything sir," J.C. said. "We're looking for Katie McClure. Does she live here?"

Before the old man could answer, their four unshaven sons tramped out onto the porch, each wearing dirty bib overalls and muddy clodhoppers with similar, odd, faces. They stared at Wally and J.C. as if they were revenuers—or worse.

The Alpha Dog of the litter spoke first, "What do yunz want?"

144

Wally took a step toward the brothers, "We unz was jist dawn tawn lookin' fer Katie McClure. Ol' geyser at the druggie store sent us out 'er."

J.C. looked at Wally in amazement.

Alpha Dog looked at his father. "Should I tell him pa?"

"What do you want her for?" the old man said, his eyes narrowed.

"She won a prize at Foodmart, over in Alvertown," J.C. said before an astonished Wally could answer. "I have to give it to her in person."

"What is it?" The old woman finally spoke.

"It's a gift certificate for fifty dollars," J.C. said.

The gothic couple and their hairy offspring looked pleased, as did Wally as evidenced by the wide grin on his face. The father and sons started to chatter among themselves.

The old woman raised her hand and the porch full of men went silent. "She works at Penelope's Dress Shop in Salem. Today she quits early, four o'clock."

Wally and J.C. thanked the McClures, climbed in the Chevy and headed west toward Salem, a twenty-minute trip.

Wally looked over at J.C. "That was quick thinking. You're learning how to handle these situations."

"Thanks, now you can pay for the gift certificate."

"First, we have to find out who Jason's secret boyfriend is," Wally said. "then we'll worry about it. If Katie's as ugly as the rest of the clan, we'll substitute a make-over from a beauty salon instead of the fifty clams."

Although Salem was a town of only 26,000 inhabitants, it was a huge metropolis compared to Madison. They found Penelope's Dress Shop in the center of the business district. Wally spotted a parking space in front of a hardware store, a few doors away. They walked to the shop. J.C. paused at the display window to look at a red dress.

"See something you'd like to try on?" Wally asked.

"Right, Wally. No, cross-dressing is more your style. You're the master of wardrobe changes. Barb's birthday is coming up and I thought—"

"Let's look inside then," Wally said, holding the door open.

An elderly woman with gray hair approached them, the hardwood floor clicking under her brisk gait. Her prominent proboscis supported jeweled, catlike eyeglasses that framed her small, beady, blue eyes. A gold chain hung from the glasses around her scrawny neck, preventing their escape. The nametag on her dress read "Beatrice." Her strained smile turned into a dignified, "May I help you?"

"A friend of mine asked me to see Katie McClure about this red dress in the window," J.C. answered.

Beatrice turned hastily on her heel, like an Army recruit performing close-order drills, and walked away.

Wally, who was facing the rear of the store, suddenly beamed with a look of pleasant surprise. "This can't be Katie, can it?"

J.C. turned around to see a gorgeous young redhead walking toward them. He forgot his manners and looked her up and down like a man buying a new car. Her short, fluffy red hair bounced with every step, as did her bountiful bosom beneath an unbuttoned, gray jacket. The gray material of her slacks didn't stop on the curves that J.C. followed upward, over her jacket and then to the red scarf around her neck. Katie certainly didn't resemble anyone else in her family. She was not only pretty, but she walked with a confident, self-assured stride. J.C. couldn't believe that she was the daughter of the couple they had just left, or even sister to the four hulking boys.

Katie stopped in front of Wally and J.C, and looked hard at their faces, studying them. "Beatrice said you were told to see me about the red dress in the window, but that's not true is it?"

Wally and J.C. looked at each other, waiting for the other to manufacture an excuse.

"Well, you see we . . . we were—"

"You were out at the house and met my family, right? You're not here to buy anything. What do you want?"

"That's not exactly true," J.C. said. "I'm interested in buying that red dress in the window, but I do have a question for you."

"Ben Hawkins said you could help us out," Wally explained.

Her face flushed, her pink cheeks a rosy contrast to her light blue eyes. "Who are you?" she asked, looking alternately at Wally and J.C. "What do you want?"

J.C. walked toward the window, gesturing for Wally and Katie to follow him. "I'm John Ducheck," he said, then hiked a thumb toward Wally. "He's Wally Gustafson. You have information that will help us."

"I'm not here to answer questions," she said. "I'm here to sell clothes."

"Well I'm here to buy that red dress," J.C. said, "and while I'm buying it, you can answer a couple of questions for us. Right?"

"Wrong," she said. "I don't have to answer anything that doesn't pertain to selling clothes." She carefully looked them over. "Are you guys cops?"

"No we're not cops, but Wally's nephew is," J.C. said. "We can have him come here and talk to you. Answer one question for us, I'll buy the dress and we'll leave. It's that simple.

Katie dug at the floor with her foot like a spooked deer. "What's the question?"

"Who was Jason Saxberg's secret boyfriend?" J.C. asked.

Her face registered surprise. She looked from J.C. to Wally and back again. "What . . . ? What do you mean secret boyfriend?"

"Ben Hawkins told us all about it Katie," Wally said. "We need the name. Was it Matthew Smith?

J.C. looked at Wally as if Wally had been withholding information from him.

Katie shook her head. "No, no, it wasn't Matthew. Why would you think that?"

"Because I saw you at Fine's Funeral Home for the reverend's visitation, that's why," Wally said, giving J.C. an informed nod.

"No, I don't know anything," she protested. "Leave me alone."

J.C. poked his finger toward Wally. "Maybe you'd like to talk to his nephew at your house. Maybe he'll ask you about drugs while he's at it."

Katie's face went white. "It wasn't Matthew."

J.C. looked at Wally. "Let's go see Paul then, Wally."

"No, no, you don't understand," Katie pleaded. "It wasn't Matthew. It was Matthew's brother, Mark. He was Jason's secret boyfriend."

"Mark?" J.C. said. "He lives in North Carolina, doesn't he?"

"He didn't up to four months ago," she said.

"How did Mark get you to go along with this arrangement?" Wally interrupted. "Was it because he knew about your drug habit and was going to tell your family?"

Katie diverted her eyes and played nervously with a charm bracelet. "Yes. The son of a bitch knew about my drug use and about the other thing also. He said he'd tell everybody if I didn't go along."

"The other thing doesn't have to be mentioned," J.C. said. "Just be honest with us, okay?"

"I told you the truth," she said. "It was Mark."

"Again," J.C. asked. "He lives in North Carolina. I don't understand."

"He comes home on weekends," she said. "A couple times a month."

"What for," Wally asked, "to see Jason?"

"Not really," she said. "He comes back mostly to pick up some coke to take back to North Carolina."

"Not to see Jason?" J.C. asked.

"No, they had broken up before Mark left home," she said. "Jason found someone else. That's why Mark left."

Wally and J.C. looked at each other with surprise.

"Who was Jason's new boyfriend?" Wally asked.

Katie looked out the window. "I don't know. He never talked about it. He seemed to be ashamed of who, or what he was."

"Would Ben Hawkins know who the new boyfriend was?" asked Wally.

"I don't know, probably. Pushers know a lot about the people they sell to," she said. Then she looked at J.C. and added knowingly, "It's for their protection, you know."

"About that red dress," J.C. said. "I'll take it in a size ten."

Katie's face brightened with relief. She went into the back room, then brought the right size of the dress to the sales counter. She folded it, put it in a box, and gift-wrapped it. J.C. paid in cash and added a twenty-dollar tip for her.

Katie followed Wally and J.C. to the door. "Will my name be brought up in this?"

"We're not cops, Katie," J.C. said. "As far as we're concerned, we didn't talk to you."

Katie smiled and looked pensive. "What about my occasional drug use, and you know, my being—"

"Like the man said, we're not cops," Wally said, handing her his card. "If you think of anything else that might help us, please call this number."

Katie took the card and stood there smiling.

Wally and J.C. got in the Chevy and headed east, toward Greenville.

"I didn't know you saw Katie at the Smith visitation," J.C. said.

"All I saw was a pretty redhead. I didn't expect her to be an offspring of the McClure's we met. It took a while for my memory to kick in. And how about you? How did you know about her using drugs?"

"I didn't," J.C. said. "I figured if I had to live in that house with that family, I might take drugs too—just to forget."

"So you figured it out, eh Sherlock?"

"Well, Katie being acquainted with Ben Hawkins kind of helped."

"We make a good team," Wally said. "We've got Jason's murderer narrowed down to two people."

"Hold the phone. Not so fast. When we suspected Matthew of his father's murder, we automatically assumed that he killed Jason first, and then his father, figuring that his father had found out about them. But Matthew doesn't have a motive to kill Jason, Mark does."

"Well, that's narrowing it down to two suspects," Wally said. "Just not the way we had it figured and maybe these murders are related in some way."

"They could be totally separate. Maybe Matthew didn't kill his father or Jason. Just because Mark was Jason's boyfriend doesn't mean he killed him. Jason's new boyfriend could have gotten jealous and killed him. The information we just got from Katie opens new doors. What about the drug connection? Maybe Fleming or Hawkins killed Jason?"

Wally stroked his chin. "Fleming was found dead. Maybe he knew too much. Hawkins is involved somehow. We have to talk to him again. He wasn't watching Fleming's back that day in the park. He was watching Fleming."

J.C. agreed. "Maybe we should tell Paul what we know."

"Not yet. Let's talk to Hawkins again, he'll know who the new boyfriend is. Maybe we'll find a drug connection. If that doesn't pan out, we'll go to Paul. That reminds me, Paul's coming over for dinner today."

"You're not going to tell him anything yet, are you?"

Wally shook his hands in a negative fashion, as if he was polishing two bowling balls at the same time. "No, but I do have some information for him about the reverend that I forgot to tell him over the weekend."

"Anything important?"

"I don't know yet," Wally said. "I'll let you know."

Chapter 22

"I forgot to tell you about my Saturday trip to Wheeling," Wally said.

The bar was empty late Tuesday morning. J.C. was bent over the sink washing glasses. His arm was pumping the mugs and eight ounces over the bristly brushes, then plunging them into clear, rinse water.

"Did you pop into one of those old cat-houses I've heard about?" J.C. asked.

Wally made a huffing sound and hiked his hands to his hips. "No, I went to the dog races and ran into Earoff Matta."

Why they call him Earoff, nobody knows. He has both ears, and intact—not like the stub Mike Tyson left on Evander Holyfield. He's a compulsive gambler and could afford it. He controlled the West Side rackets, providing him a cornucopia of money from numbers and illegal poker machines. Earoff loved money, but he had no sense of humor. Wally had asked him once if he had a sister named Whatsa. He didn't laugh.

"What'd he have to say?"

"I was talking to him about handicapping the fifth race when I brought up the subject about the reverend being shot. He didn't seem too surprised."

"Why not? Did you ask?"

"Yeah, I asked. He said he knew about the reverend's gambling and peculiar lifestyle when he was away from home."

"What lifestyle away from home?" J.C. asked.

"He said he saw the reverend in disguise in Atlantic City with a younger man."

"In disguise? The reverend used disguises?"

"Yeah. This time Earoff said he was dressed as a rabbi."

"That's funny. Did Earoff hear what they said?"

"No, but they were having a heated discussion. It had something to do with money," Wally said.

"What about this man he was with, did he give a description?"

"You bet," Wally said. "Earoff said he looked like Pee Wee Herman."

"He wouldn't be hard to spot," J.C. said, stacking clean glasses under the bar, "if we can narrow the candidates to twenty. Good work Wally. I'll put you up for promotion."

"I'm retired," Wally replied, "You can't get any more promoted than that."

The phone rang. J.C. grabbed a bar towel and dried his hands. He picked up the receiver on the fourth ring.

"Hello."

"Is this John Charles Ducheck?" The voice sounded female and agitated.

"Yes. May I—?"

"This is Katie McClure. I have to talk to you."

J.C. could hear the fear in her voice; she sounded like she was on the verge of crying.

"What's the Matter? What happened Katie?" J.C.'s face contorted in concern. He mouthed "Katie" to let Wally know whom he was talking to.

"I was stopped by a man, a masked man. He threatened me."

J.C. couldn't believe what he was hearing. Why would someone threaten Katie? Were they getting close to finding some answers on the Saxberg case or was it something else?

"When—where?" J.C. asked, his facial expression reflected Katie's fear.

"Last night; about nine-fifteen. I was coming home after work when a truck cut me off. He forced me off the road."

"A truck?" J.C. thought about the truck that tried to ambush him on the way home from the community college. Wally picked up on the words.

"What kind of truck?" J.C. asked.

"I don't know . . . a dark one. Anyway the masked man wanted to know what you and your friend wanted with me."

"What did you tell him?"

"At first I was mad. I told him it was none of his business. But then—" She started to cry, then composed herself. "Then he pulled a shiny gun from his pocket."

"A shiny gun?" J.C. nodded to Wally.

"Yeah, a pistol. It was very shiny. I got scared. I told him everything. I thought he was going to kill me; I couldn't help it. I would have called earlier but my parents—"

"That's all right Katie, as long as you're all right. He didn't hurt you, did he?"

"No, just scared the hell out of me. When I told him about Hawkins, you know about his knowing who Saxberg's new boyfriend was, he left."

"I'm sorry this happened to you Katie; I didn't think you would be involved." J.C. looked as if he had lost his last token on a bus to nowhere. "If there's anything—"

"It's not your fault. It's this nut with a mask. He needs to be put away."

"I've got to go now, but I promise you that I'll do everything I can to find out who he is." J.C. heard a faint whimpering and then a sigh. "Thanks again." He hung up.

"Did I hear what I think I heard?" Wally asked.

"We've got to get to Hawkins and warn him that someone with a gun wants to talk to him."

"If this masked man wants Hawkins that bad, he must know an awful lot."

"We'll have to talk to him first then." J.C. wondered to what extremes this nut would go to keep them from finding out who he was. Would he threaten Barb or hurt her?

#

After lunch, Wally picked J.C. up at Ducheck's and they drove to Ben Hawkins' address.

The houses on Luce Avenue once stood proud with energy derived from the happy, working class families that lived there. Now, they seemed to sulk in disappointment from negligence and abandonment.

Hawkins' two-storey shack stood between two boarded-up houses that had aged, barely visible "For Sale" signs stuck in the high grass of their front yards.

Wally pulled into the driveway and parked near the garage. "No lights. He's probably not home."

"Let's try knocking," J.C. said, jumping out of the truck.

They both walked up seven steps to the porch, to the glassless, solid wood door.

J.C. pounded on the portal. "Hawkins, Ben Hawkins. It's Wally and J.C. We've got to ask you a few questions."

Wally tried to look in the front window. "He's got plywood covering the window. Those drapes are painted on to look like a normal window."

"Let's go around back," J.C. said walking down the steps.

Wally followed J.C. along the right side of the house. The wood in the side windows was also painted with fake curtains. "Shit!" Wally yelped as he stepped on a rake. "Why didn't you tell me there was a rake here? The son of a bitch hit me in the noggin'"

"I thought you'd see it," J.C. said, stifling a laugh. "It's right on the walk."

"You were right in front of me. Let me know next time."

They made their way to the back of the house. A small porch led to the back door.

J.C. climbed the five wooden steps and knocked on the door, trying to look in. "Nothing. This one's boarded up too." He looked over at the garage. "Let's check out the garage, Wally."

Wally rubbed his forehead as he followed J.C.'s footsteps to the garage.

"The door's open," J.C. said. "Let's see what's inside." He pulled out a small, pocket flashlight and shone it around the garage.

"Over there," Wally said, tapping J.C. on his right shoulder. "Shine the light over there—to the right."

J.C. shone the light where Wally pointed.

"Notice anything peculiar?" Wally asked.

"Looks like a normal garage to me."

Wally pointed at the bench. "His toolbox is gone. I saw it on the bench when we were here the other day."

"Are you sure?"

"Absolutely. I noticed it because it was a new Craftsman tool box. It stuck out like a sore thumb in this dirty garage."

J.C. shone the flashlight slowly around the garage. "Maybe he's gone. Maybe he took off before he ended up like Fleming."

"Could be," Wally said. "Maybe he was getting ready to go when we talked to him."

"He did seem nervous. Kind of jittery, like he was being watched or something."

"I'm starting to feel the same way myself. Let's get the hell out of here."

"I agree," J.C. said, walking toward the door, shining the light on the floor as they left the garage. "Maybe it's time to tell Paul. Fleming ended up in a garbage bag and now Hawkins has disappeared. What next?"

"Let's drive to Paul's house now."

J.C. agreed and they turned to leave.

"Hold it right there!"

J.C. looked up. A uniformed police officer was blocking their exit.

#

Paul sat at his desk wondering where Nuggets' aunt, Emily Watkins, had gone. He had done the usual preliminary checking with the County Recorder of Deeds, City Tax Office, voter registration and women's clubs' memberships, all to no avail.

Paul remembered Nuggets saying his aunt had lived on Leeds Avenue. He picked up the phone and speed-dialed the second precinct. He asked for, and was switched to, the desk sergeant. Paul had done several favors for him before and asked if he could spare a couple of officers for a few hours.

"I can manage that. What for?"

"I'm trying to locate a woman who used to live on Leeds Avenue. I don't have her former address. Maybe a neighbor . . . ?"

The sergeant sighed. "Leeds is about twelve blocks long."

"I'm not in any hurry. Whenever you get time."

"We're a little busy, but I'll get on it."

Paul had given the sergeant her name and was thanking him when an officer walked up to his desk.

"Your uncle and his friend are downstairs."

Chapter 23

After the third knock, Paul opened the door. The pungent smell of beer and whiskey enveloped Wally and J.C. let them know it wasn't a good time to explain why they were working behind Paul's back on the Saxberg case.

"Fuck's the matter with you guys?" Paul slurred, his eyes swollen and glassy. "Out there playing detective. Made me look like a real asshole." He turned around and waved them in as he staggered into the living room. "Had to explain to the boss again. He was pissed."

"Is that why we were held captive 'til six o'clock?" Wally asked.

"No, I'm responsible for that. Have a seat," Paul said disappearing into the kitchen. He could be heard saying, "Time for a drink."

The room looked like it hadn't been cleaned since Paul's divorce, eight years ago. The carpet was threadbare in a path from the sunken couch to the kitchen, probably from retrieving six-packs.

Wally plopped on a wooden chair to the right of the couch and sat down. J.C. snuggled in a plush, dark green recliner on the other side.

Paul returned from the kitchen with a fresh six-pack and switched the TV on to a replay of an old Steeler's game. "Help yourselves, guys," he said as he pulled three cans of I.C. Light from their plastic neckties and slid them over the cluttered coffee table almost knocking over a fifth of Bellows. "So, tell me. What the hell were you guys thinking?" He grabbed a beer, popped the tab and slumped into the swayback couch.

J.C. looked at Wally as if to say "this visit is a big mistake," but Paul was family. He was the only one that could help, the only one who would understand why they did what they did and help them find Jason's murderer without getting themselves involved any further with the police. After all, their list of "felonies and misdemeanors" was growing. They withheld information and evidence, blackmailed Jimmy Restivo, and talked to Ralph Fleming before he was murdered. J.C. hoped Paul would understand and help them—if he could stay sober long enough.

Wally seemed to be thinking the same thing. He sat solemn, apparently mulling over his choice of words. "Paul, I'm sorry this was a bad reflection on you but we need your help."

"You seem to have been doing a pretty good job so far," Paul said. "You've been snooping around a lot of places and getting in trouble. Even arrested."

"It's more than that," Wally said. "It's getting dangerous."

Paul sat up straight. A look of concern covered his face; his eyes seemed to focus. He switched the TV off. "You guys in trouble?"

J.C. tried to keep his voice slow and distinct. "Well, not really . . . not yet, but—"

"Spill it," Paul said. "What's the problem?"

Paul's head went back and forth from Wally to J.C. as each took turns telling how they got Jimmy Restivo to tell them about Ralph Fleming, how Fleming wouldn't talk to them, but suddenly changed his mind a day later and how they found Ben Hawkins hiding in the creek bed.

"What did Fleming tell you?" Paul interrupted.

Wally explained about Saxberg's secret boyfriend and how he had an arrangement with a red-headed closet lesbian. Paul really perked up when J.C. said that the secret boyfriend was Mark Smith, the reverend's son. Wally explained how they found the redhead thanks to information supplied by Hawkins who was now apparently missing.

"He's probably scared," Paul said. "Whoever killed Fleming is after Hawkins, and he knows it." Paul looked at Wally. "Are you sure he's missing?"

"His tools are missing and no one's home. That's when the police came.

"Why'd you go there in the first place?" Paul asked.

J.C. got Paul's attention with a hand wave. "Because Jason Saxberg broke up with Mark and found a new boyfriend. Hawkins knows who it is."

Paul sat back against the tilted back of the couch. "Sounds like Mr. Hawkins is the key." He looked at Wally. "I'll have a patrol car drive past Hawkins' house every few hours." Paul flipped a small notebook over to Wally. "Write down his address."

"You'll help us then?" J.C. asked.

"Regretfully," Paul said with a hint of enthusiasm. "I have more time now that Gerri hit the road. Now get the hell out of here."

#

A dark truck quietly idled across the street from Paul's house. The masked occupant waited patiently, his finger on the trigger of a stainless steel Beretta 9mm semi-automatic pistol.

Wally and J.C. left Paul to the fourth quarter of the Steeler rerun; both seemed relieved that Paul was now in their corner.

Paul had a large front yard, mostly grass with a border of six evergreens next to the sidewalk. A three-foot hedge framed the 75-foot walkway to the sidewalk.

J.C. was listening to Wally complain about the ink stains on his fingers leftover from being fingerprinted when he noticed the idling dark truck. He kept his eyes locked on the vehicle. When he saw a silvery reflection from inside the cab, probably caused by the moon, he tackled Wally and drove him over the hedge. The sound of a gunshot pierced the stillness of the night; its flash partially illuminated the dark street.

J.C. landed on top of Wally, knocking the wind out of him. He couldn't talk or move but managed a wheezing sound. J.C. dragged him out of the line of fire behind an evergreen. Kneeling low, J.C. pushed a branch aside to see if the shooter was getting out of the truck.

Another shot rang out, hitting the front of Paul's house, between the doorbell and the porch light.

J.C. turned around. He saw Paul standing in the doorway, "He's after Paul!"

Wally tried to get up, but couldn't. He was still trying to catch his breath; his face contorted more from fear than pain.

J.C. yelled for Paul to stay in the house, but it was too late. Paul stepped out onto the porch. That's when the last report rang out.

J.C. heard the shot that seemed to echo through a slow-motion picture of Paul falling back against the doorframe of the house, his head lurching forward, then back. Blood appeared, slowly dripping down the white, aluminum siding of the house. Paul slowly followed the red streaks until he was seated on the porch. Then, as if being tugged by a string, he fell over to his left side.

The roar of an engine and the screeching of tires on asphalt brought J.C. back to real time. He watched the dark truck speed down the block. Wally had regained his breath and senses. He was frantically crawling toward the house. J.C. helped Wally to his feet and they both scrambled to the porch where Paul lay.

J.C. instinctively took charge. Perhaps in his forgotton past he had first aid or medical training. Paul had a very minor flesh wound to the left shoulder. He also realized that his unconsciousness was probably alcohol-induced, not due to the injury.

He took off his shirt and handed it to Wally. "Rip this into strips." He applied pressure to the wound with the palm of his right hand, slowing the flow of blood. Wally ripped a three-inch wide strip and handed it to J.C. He folded it into a pad and covered the wound with it. The next strip he tied around the patch, partially securing it.

"What the hell," Paul said, suddenly flinging his arms, pushing J.C. away. "What are you doing?"

"You've been shot!" Wally said. "He's trying to help you."

Paul's head slowly turned to look at his shoulder, his eyes trying to focus. "Yeah, I heard the gunshot. Who would—"

"Don't know. Someone in a dark truck. I think the same guy that ambushed me when I was coming home from the community college."

"Someone's either following you or knows where you're going." Paul said. He seemed to sober up now. "Someone knew you were going to Hawkins' house and called the police, the same person who waited for you across the street."

J.C. wrapped another strip around the bandage to keep it from moving. "Sounds like you might suspect who it is."

"Just a hunch—for now."

#

The early morning sun shone through the east window in the records area, striking the black file cabinets, causing them to look charcoal. Paul thumbed through the D's looking for J.C.'s file and the fingerprints that would be attached. He knew he would have to obtain a set of prints from Nuggets as well to be sent in also. Why not a set for J.C. at the same time? After all, people make mistakes. Maybe A.F.I.S. overlooked something when J.C.'s prints were sent in the first time.

Paul found the file and opened it. It was a small file, containing only interviews of the attempts on his life. He scanned the file, not finding the page he was looking for. He went through the file again, this time slower. No prints. He checked the routing slip to see who had signed the file out last so he could talk to him. The routing slip was gone. Paul became agitated. Then he thought that it wasn't that unusual; routing slips had fallen off before, and besides, he could get J.C.'s prints the same time he got Nuggets' and send them in together.

Chapter 24

Jaunting down the sidewalk toward Ducheck's, Wally seemed happy, like a kid leaving school for summer recess. J.C. noticed Wally's new vigor as he entered the bar, attributing his vitality to being on board with his nephew and the fact that Paul had survived last night's attack. His minor flesh wound, a scratch really, would have sent lesser men to the worker's compensation rolls, but not Paul. He asked to remain on duty and the commander agreed.

Four men, who had worked the midnight shift on the *Batteries* at the local coke plant, were sitting at a table, looking spent, replenishing their bodily fluids with pitchers of Coors Light draft, their drawn faces reflecting a hard, hot, night's work.

Wally nodded in recognition as he passed their table.

"Did you talk to Paul yet?" J.C. shouted over the Channel 11 morning news.

"Not yet, I thought I'd wait 'til I got here."

Wally pulled out his cell-phone and poked in Paul's number at the station. J.C. turned the volume down on the

TV. Talking to Paul, Wally's facial expressions shifted between hope and disappointment.

J.C. hung on every word of the one-sided conversation, like an expectant father listening to the delivery room doctor, until Wally hung up.

"What did he say?" J.C. asked.

Wally motioned J.C. to the end of the bar, away from the table where the workmen were seated. "Paul said Hawkins hasn't been seen. He has officers talking to his known acquaintances. He's doing this on his own because he can't justify a case to his superiors and can't get the needed manpower."

J.C. leaned on the bar, closing the gap between himself and Wally. "I heard you say, 'How long will it take?' What did you mean?"

"I wanted to know how long it would take to find Hawkins. Paul didn't know. Said he would do his best."

"What about a search warrant?"

"He can't get one," Wally said. "No probable cause."

Wally and J.C. sat silent for a moment, thinking about their situation, and then, as if on cue, looked at each other with Cheshire cat grins.

Wally leaned closer. "Call Nuggets, we don't have to have probable cause."

J.C. walked to the wall phone at the end of the bar and made the call. He slowly walked back to where Wally was sitting.

"How are we going to break into Hawkins' house in broad daylight?" J.C. thought about how he couldn't explain another breaking and entering charge to Barb. She understood the last time. What about a repeat performance? "The police are watching the place."

Wally stroked his chin. He looked up with steady eyes, as if he was taking a picture with his mind. "We'll pull the Chevy into the garage. It's empty, right?"

"Right, I didn't think of that. The abandoned houses on

both sides of Hawkins' will shield us from neighbors. What about getting into the house?"

"I've got a crowbar and a three-pound hammer in the truck. That should get us in anywhere."

"What do we look for?"

"I don't know," Wally said half-heartedly. "Anything that will help us, I guess."

Nuggets sauntered from around the corner of the back room and walked behind the bar. J.C. talked to him for a minute before surrendering his watch. Wally and J.C. left with a plan.

Driving to Hawkins' house, they discussed possibilities as to why he had left town in such a hurry.

Wally brought up the possibility that Hawkins had killed Fleming, because he wanted more action with the drug trade, and went on a vacation to let things cool off.

J.C. thought that Hawkins knew they were getting close to finding Jason's murderer and he didn't want to identify Jason's new secret boyfriend—maybe someone influential— maybe the same person who killed Fleming.

They both figured drugs had entered into the equation somehow with Hawkins' disappearance.

Wally turned onto Luce Avenue. He drove slowly, looking for any signs of police or plainclothes detectives surveilling the area. When he determined that the area was clear, Wally darted into Hawkins' driveway, coming to a dusty stop in front of the garage. J.C. hopped out of the truck and flung open the garage doors. He waited for Wally to pull into its dark interior and then quickly closed the doors, concealing their presence.

J.C. shone his small flashlight on the floor as they made their way to a rear door on the right side of the garage. Wally cracked it open and, after checking the driveway and street, they hunkered down behind yucca and lily plants before dashing 30 feet to the rear porch.

Wally got to the back door first. He dropped the crowbar

and hammer on a rusty metal chair and knocked. J.C. peered around the corner of the house and scanned the neighborhood and street. After knocking three times, Wally picked up the crowbar and attempted to open the door. He tried to get leverage by prying the end of the bar between the stubborn portal and frame, but it wouldn't budge.

"Must be reinforced inside," Wally said, looking at the crowbar in disgust. "This won't open it."

"How about the window?" J.C. pointed at the double-hung window a few feet left of the door. "We can open the window and pry the plywood off."

Wally hustled over with the bar. "We'll have to break a pane of glass to get to the latch. Go back in the garage and get me a couple of rags."

In less than a minute, J.C. was back with the rags. Wally wrapped three of them around his elbow. Wally broke the pane of glass above the locking latch with a deft blow from his rag-protected elbow. He unlocked it and J.C. raised the window.

"This will do the trick," Wally said, wedging the bar between the windowsill and the plywood. A few yanks on the bar and the plywood was peeling off the frame. Wally could only pry at the bottom half of the window as the two halves were now together, at the top.

"Son of a bitch," he said, "I can't reach the upper part to get a bite on it."

J.C. took the crowbar and sat on the windowsill, twisting his body in an awkward position to get the prybar above the bottom half of the window. After a few tugs and jerks, the cover was opening up, but not enough to free the plywood from the window frame. "Maybe we can push it open."

"It's worth a try," Wally said, pulling J.C. to his feet. "Let's both try it with the bar."

Wally and J.C. used their combined weight to push the plywood back as far as they could, but it was still firmly secured to the top third of the frame.

"I think there's enough room for me to squeeze in at the bottom," J.C. said, pointing to a twenty-inch opening. "Those nails will have to be hammered back or I'll shred my skin to ribbons."

Wally handed J.C. the hammer. "You've got the right idea. That's the only way we're going to get into this fortress."

J.C. hammered the points of the nails until they were pushed back into the wood. He then slowly, methodically, and in yoga-like postures, squeezed through the narrow opening. He unlocked the back door for Wally. J.C. turned the kitchen light on and they quickly pushed the plywood cover back in place and secured it by tapping the nails into the frame.

The place was a mess. The kitchen sink, countertops, table, and other horizontal surfaces were covered with dirty pots, pans, dishes, and silverware. A doorway leading to the basement was at the end of the kitchen. J.C. located a tandem light switch, flipped one on, and the stairs were illuminated. He turned on the other one and a flood of light burst up the stairwell.

"What's he got down there?" J.C. asked, retreating. "Floodlights?"

"I think he's into agriculture," Wally said, grabbing J.C.'s arm. "Let's go down and see."

Wally and J.C. descended the stairs to a marijuana field that covered the entire basement. Three rows of tables, benches, and assorted four-foot platforms supported marijuana plants growing in containers of all shapes and sizes. They were illuminated by grow lights that hung from the basement rafters. Plants were also on the floor, lit by fixtures attached to the undersides of the tables, producing a two-storey pot farm.

"Holy mackerel," Wally said. "There's enough weed down here to sustain all the rock bands in L.A."

They went back upstairs to the kitchen and into the dining room, or in this case, the wrapping room. A spacious table, probably used for family gatherings in happier times, was being used to wrap the funny cigarettes. There was a scale, a mechanical cigarette wrapper and all the paraphernalia needed to produce enough joints for the entire neighborhood—and then some.

"Looks like he took some product with him," Wally said, pointing at an empty metal bin, about the size of a breadbox, next to the wrapping machine. "This is the input side of the wrapping process."

"He must have really been in a hurry not to take all of it."

"Either he's scared shitless, or he's on a vacation. I'll bet he's not on vacation."

"Looks that way," J.C. said, reaching around the doorway. He turned the light on in the living room.

A big-screen TV and a modern oak bar took up most of the space in the 12x12 room. The frayed and discolored furniture consisted of a couch and two matching upholstered chairs. A large coffee table sat in front of the couch, littered with glasses, beer cans, and ashtrays. The bar looked like an elevated coffee table.

Wally stopped to look at a stain, the color of rancid animal fat, on the white, upholstered couch. "Looks like someone lost control of their bladder."

"The chairs aren't much different," J.C. said, avoiding contact with the furniture and walking to the stairway near the front door.

They climbed the stairs and entered the first room on the left, a bedroom. The end table and dresser drawers were open and empty. The closet was half empty, only the winter clothes remained.

They walked down the hall. J.C. peeled off into the bathroom. He checked the drawers and medicine cabinet and noticed that the toothbrush and paste were missing.

Wally had already entered a small room at the end of the hall.

J.C. followed him in. "Looks like he converted the bedroom into a den."

On the left, in the center of the wall, a large oak desk was cluttered with papers, junk mail, and old bills. The drawers were open and empty. Wally looked through the papers on top of the desk. "I'll check out these papers. J.C., see what you can come up with."

"Looks like he isn't on vacation," J.C. said, looking at the empty drawers. "Hawkins took what he could in a hurry, even his toothbrush." He was browsing through the titles of some of the books on an upright, wooden bookcase on the right wall, pushing some aside to get a better look at them when one of the books got hung up on something. "Looky here," he said, smiling at Wally. He pointed at the empty space between the books.

"What's that?"

"A wall safe. It's empty, proves he left for good, doesn't it?"

"Looks that way," Wally said, throwing down some papers on the desk. "Nothin' here. Check around some more."

"What are those trophies for?" J.C. asked.

A shelf, a few feet from the desktop, held four gold-colored trophies on walnut stands with an inscribed plate on each.

Wally picked one up, tilted it for better light, and read it. "Third place, six-hundred meter, Camp Perry." He looked at J.C. "It's for target shooting."

There was an old picture hanging above the trophies that caught Wally's eye. He lifted it off its nail and studied it.

J.C. looked over Wally's shoulder at the picture. Young boys were standing together, holding rifles at port arms. "Anyone you know?"

"Yep." Wally pointed to faces on the dusty glass. "That's Matthew here, Mark, these two are the commander's kids, Hawkins, and that—" Wally pointed with a deliberate finger. "That's Jason Saxberg."

J.C. leaned closer. "They were on a rifle team together. Matthew and Mark knew Jason very well, didn't they?"

"Yeah, I guess so. I almost forgot about the rifle team. It was part of the Boy Scout troop that the United Methodist Church sponsored."

J.C. pointed at the picture, resting his digit on a small, pointy-faced boy. "Who's that?"

"I don't know." Wally said, rubbing his chin. "He looks familiar though. Can't place his face."

"It'll come to you. Let's get the hell out of here. Call Paul. Tell him we'll meet him for lunch."

Chapter 25

"I can't today," Paul said, "I'm on my way to meet Councilman Martinet for lunch at the Belle Nova."

Wally had called to make arrangements to talk to Paul. He and J.C. were both eager to tell him what they had discovered.

Wally hesitated. "We'll see you later at Ducheck's then. Okay?"

"Fine," Paul said, pulling into the restaurant parking lot. "See you there."

A quaint little place, the restaurant sat in a remote setting two miles out of town on a country road that led to Farmington, a coal-mining patch. During the day, the dining room provided an out-of-the-way meeting place for attorneys and politicians avoiding the sunshine law and, in the evenings, the bar provided a rendezvous for those eager to cheat on their spouses.

Paul waited only a few minutes for Ted and greeted him as he exited his new Cadillac. They talked about the weather and other unimportant issues while walking to the restaurant. Ted led the way to a corner booth in the rear.

A pretty, young waitress, who seemed to know Ted very well, took their lunch order.

As soon as the waitress left, Ted asked, "Do you remember Officer Mike Fahey?"

"Yeah, vaguely. He retired some time ago, didn't he?"

"Fifteen years ago. I had a talk with him last night, a confidential talk, okay?" He looked at Paul, waiting for an agreeable sign. "He doesn't want his name mentioned about this, understood?"

"Understood." Paul slid toward the edge of his chair.

"Murdock was chief at the time. He came walking through the squad room grabbed Fahey as his driver. They drove to Julius Butterfield's house."

"Is that the Butterfield that had the men's store? Juliano's, on fourteenth?"

"That's the one." Ted leaned forward and hunched over the table, keeping the conversation confidential. "Anyway, Fahey was told to wait outside, on the front door stoop."

"So? Maybe he had some personal stuff to discuss."

Ted shook his head. "No, something else. It started to rain and Fahey went into the house to keep dry. He overheard Julius' son, Troy, tell the chief that Reverend Smith had sexually molested him."

Ted winked at Paul and sat straight in his chair; the waitress had come with their food. Paul couldn't wait to hear the end of Ted's story. After some casual flirting by Ted, the waitress left.

Ted hunched over the table again. "He heard the chief say that he would take care of it. Fahey slipped outside, knowing he had heard too much. He acted as if he had been outside the whole time when the chief came out."

"What happened then?"

"Fahey said he drove the chief to the United Methodist Church's Parsonage. He went in by himself for about half an hour, then Fahey drove him back to the Butterfield's."

"Did the chief say anything about why he had gone to the Butterfield's and then to the reverend's house?"

"Fahey said that the chief passed it off as a misunderstanding, that Butterfield had jumped to conclusions, and that everything was settled. There was no complaint."

"Didn't Fahey ask about the misunderstanding?" Paul asked.

"I asked him about that. He said he was afraid of being fired, so he kept his mouth shut."

"At that time, it was probably the best thing to do," Paul said. "The job was extremely command and control, if you know what I mean."

"It must have been hard for Fahey to have kept quiet so long."

"He was afraid, and probably forgot about it. By the way, how did you know to go to him?"

"Just lucky," Ted said. "I thought I'd ask a few retired cops, ones that I knew and had confidence in me. Fahey and I grew up together and he knows I wouldn't get him involved. Right?"

"I forgot his name already. Thanks for the information Ted, it'll really help."

Paul grabbed the check and they left the restaurant talking about baseball and how the Pirates would fare in the playoffs.

# #

Paul headed for Ducheck's to tell Wally and J.C. about his meeting with Ted Martinet. He arrived after a twenty-five minute drive.

Nuggets stood behind the bar. He motioned with his head that Wally and J.C. were in the back room.

"I'll take a round back and save you the trouble," Paul said.

"Okay, but it's no bother."

Paul grabbed a bag of chips off the display at the end of the bar. "Give me an extra glass too. The grease on these chips cuts down the foam."

"Sure does," Nuggets said, popping the cap from an I.C. Light. "Anything else?"

"This'll hold us for a while."

Paul walked toward the back room. As soon as he turned the corner and out of sight, he put the tray down on a table, took out his handkerchief and wrapped it around the empty glass. He put it in his pocket, picked up the tray, the glasses clinking against the bottles like little church bells, and walked to the back booth.

"Here you go guys. Bottoms up."

Wally had come in half an hour earlier and had written down some facts that he wanted to talk to Paul about.

Paul restocked the table and filled his glass. Paul and J.C. listened as Wally started to tell his story. "What, you broke in his house? What are you, fucking crazy? Don't you know there's a nutcase out there with a gun?"

"We had to be certain," J.C. said. "We had to know if Hawkins had left town."

Wally explained that Hawkins had emptied his safe and had taken his tools plus a few clothes. "I know he's afraid of someone. He left like a shot; he even left his marijuana plants."

"Marijuana plants!"

J.C. knew Paul was upset, so he took his time describing Hawkins' basement.

Paul looked at Wally and J.C. with curious contempt. Meanwhile, under the table, he removed his MasterCard he had taken from his wallet and wiped it clean with the tablecloth. "Did anyone see you?"

"No," J.C. said. "We made sure the street was clear and pulled into his garage."

Paul held the MasterCard by the edges and handed it to J.C. "Do you have one of these?"

J.C. took the card and looked at it. "No. I'm in debt already. I don't need to dig myself in deeper." He handed the card back to Paul.

Paul took it by its edges and slid it into his shirt pocket.

"So, he left town," Paul said, remembering what the question was. "I don't see any connection here."

"He left town all right," J.C. said. "He was packing his Bravada when we got there. In order to get rid of us, he told us where to find the redhead, Katie McClure."

"That's a connection between Hawkins and Fleming. Where's the connection between Hawkins and Jason?"

"We found a picture of Hawkins' Boy Scout troop shooting team." Wally said, his hands on his hips in a confrontational pose. "Guess who was in it?"

Paul said, "I haven't the foggiest."

"To name a few," Wally said, "the reverend's kids and Jason Saxberg."

Paul looked surprised. He picked up his mug and took a large draw, draining it by half. "The reverend's kids too, huh? That might be a motive for the reverend's murder." Paul told Wally and J.C. about what Councilman Martinet had told him at lunch, but didn't reveal his name.

"Wow, I'm getting dizzy," J.C. said. "This whole thing is intertwined like a big ball of messy facts, a puzzle with the pieces strewn all over the place."

"I'll talk to Troy Butterfield tomorrow," Paul said. "Maybe he'll shed some light on this."

Wally seemed interested. "Did Martinet give you any info' on Troy?"

"Yeah," Paul replied, "Could be the reverend sexually abused the kid and it was covered up by ex-Chief Murdock."

Wally looked like his mental gears were clicking. "Can you get me a recent picture of Troy?"

"Maybe," Paul said. "Why?"

"I don't know," Wally said. "I'm not sure. Troy may have been with the reverend in Atlantic City. I'd like to find out."

Chapter 26

July 25th was turning out to be a warm, pleasant day, free from burglaries, rapes, domestic disputes, and other assorted societal enigmas; a good start for Paul. It was 10:00 a.m., and the shops on the East Side that survived the era of plant closings were open for business. Paul was headed for one of them—Juliano's.

Paul drove onto Marne Avenue to 14th Street. Troy Butterfield's statement would be another confirmation of the reverend's abuse, sexual or otherwise. He needed to substantiate a motive for the reverend's murder and it looked as if abuse would be the starting point. Paul thought Matthew was still the prime suspect, but he'd have to obtain a lot more concrete evidence for the district attorney to issue an arrest warrant.

Juliano's was a men's store specializing in upscale formal wear, but had started selling furniture as well to stay in business. In May, the place was jammed with blemished high school boys getting fitted for their high school proms. Today the store was empty.

A gray-haired man in his late fifties, wearing a baggy, black suit, limped up to Paul and forced a fake entrepreneurial smile.

"Can I help you sir?" he said in a deep, gravely, voice— probably a result of Red Lung from years of working in the steel mills.

"Troy Butterfield?" Paul asked, noticing the salesman's displeasure that he wasn't a customer.

"He's in the back," he said, gesturing with a gnarled hand toward an office at the rear of the store.

Paul walked briskly to the area the salesman had indicated and stood at a sales counter in front of the office. The door was open. A man with a slim, triangular face and slicked back dark hair was seated at a large oak desk working on a computer.

"Excuse me. Troy Butterfield?"

"Yes," he said, looking up with large, soulful eyes. "How may I help you?"

"I'd like to talk to you about Reverend Smith," Paul said, flashing his tin. "I'm Detective Andrews and I'm investigating his murder."

Troy pushed the computer keyboard to the side. He looked annoyed.

"I'd like to ask you a few questions, that's all."

Butterfield stood up. He was a short man, about 5' 3", and frail. He was wearing a dark gray, double-breasted suit. It looked identical to the one that was on a store mannequin. He waved Paul in the office and motioned to an upholstered leather chair. "Have a seat, Detective."

"I'd like you to corroborate some information I've gathered about Reverend Smith."

"And what might that be?" Troy said, grabbing a cigarette from a wrinkled pack on his desk.

Paul hesitated. The furrows deepened on his face. "I've found out from a number of people that Reverend Smith abused them, sometimes sexually."

"I don't know what I can do for you?" Troy said, clicking his lighter nervously, trying to light his cigarette, "I mean, why come to me about it?"

"I know you were abused," Paul said, letting Troy think that he had dug up a non-existent report to that effect. "Murdock was chief at that time, wasn't he?"

Troy puffed hard on his cigarette trying to keep it lit. "What time . . . what are you talking about?"

"Look, I know what happened. I don't want to publicize it and, if you help me, I'll keep you from testifying in court. All I want to know is what happened."

"Why do you want to know?" Troy said, rocking in his chair, flicking his ashes toward the ashtray and missing it. "Why talk to me?"

Paul tried for thirty minutes to convince Troy that he was on his side, that it would benefit not only him, but also all the others that were abused, to tell what had happened. It wasn't until Paul made a connection to Jason Saxberg that Troy acquiesced.

"I'm trying to establish motive in Reverend Smith's murder. I believe it's sexual abuse and related to Jason Saxberg's murder as well. I just want to know if it's true."

Troy walked over and closed the door to his office. He suddenly seemed more aggressive. "Yes, it's true, but I thought it was to be kept secret. How did you know?"

"It's still a secret as far as I'm concerned. How did this happen? Was it at Sunday School?"

"That's where it started," Troy said with a sigh, as if he wanted to forget it. "Then later in the rifle team. It got worse when we went on bivouac one summer."

"Do you know of any others that the reverend abused?"

"No," Troy said, looking down and to the left, a sign Paul had seen many times before when people had lied. "I don't think so."

"How long did this go on?"

"A couple of years, maybe." His eyes were starting to well up; his lip quivered.

"What other boys went on bivouac with you?"

"I can't remember all of them right now. Can I call you later?"

"Sure," Paul said, handing Troy his card.

Paul thanked him for Troy's help and left. He knew that another motive for the reverend's murder might come to light, but for now, sexual abuse was the predominant one.

Chapter 27

Wally had a hunch and couldn't wait to follow up on it. He had already taken care of his pigeons, eaten breakfast, washed his Chevy, and cleaned the kitchen by 11:00 a.m. when Paul called. He told Wally about the interview he had with Troy Butterfield, that Troy was a member of the rifle team and had admitted that the reverend was sexually abusive.

A mental snapshot of the picture in Hawkins' den suddenly focused in Wally's consciousness. "You wouldn't happen to have a photo of him, would you?"

"No."

"What'd he look like?"

"Small guy, frail, dark hair. He has a pointed face."

"Thanks, See you later," Wally said and hung up the receiver.

Wally quickly formulated a plan that he thought would tie up some loose ends, but he needed help. He called J.C. and asked him to be available after lunch.

"What for? Where are we going?"

"Fourteenth Street," Wally replied. "You're going to be my photographer."

"Huh?"

"I'll tell you on the way over, just look like a photographer."

\#

Wally arrived at Ducheck's sporting a gray, pin-striped business suit and black patent leather shoes. He had his curly gray hair slicked back in waves like Donald Duck's Uncle Gladstone. He has used an obnoxious tonic that smelled like shoe polish and Alberto VO5—or maybe it was his new aftershave.

"What're you doing, posing as a photographer?" J.C. asked, looking at Wally's ancient Polaroid Land Camera that hung around his neck by a frayed, nubby leather strap.

"Troy Butterfield," Wally said, patting the camera. "If things work out the way I think they will, this lens will bring the reverend's murder into focus."

"The reverend's murder?" J.C. asked. "I thought we were working on Jason's murder?"

"We are. I think they're related."

Wally explained what Paul had told him over the phone about his interview with Troy and his relationship with the rifle team and the abuse. He said the boy in the team photo that Wally didn't recognize might be Troy Butterfield.

"He could've been Jason's new boyfriend," Wally said. "This could be the break we've been waiting for."

"But why do we need this photo?"

"If I'm right, it'll connect Troy to the reverend."

"I'll be right back." J.C. ran from behind the bar, dashed upstairs and came back with a small, silver camera. "We'll take this."

"What's that?"

"It's a digital camera, the kind a real photographer would have."

"I need to have an instant copy. I can't wait to develop it."

"I can print it out in seconds," J.C. said, "and besides, a real photographer would have a modern camera. You want to pass as a publicity man, don't you?"

Wally acquiesced and they headed for Juliano's.

Ten minutes later, they were on 14th Street approaching the store. Wally passed it up and parked a block away.

"I get it," J.C. said. "You don't want the truck to be seen. A publicity man wouldn't have an old truck. Right?"

"Right," Wally said, exiting the truck. He fed the parking meter and they walked toward Juliano's.

Sprouts of grass and weeds were growing where multitudes of footfalls once trampled the cracked and uneven walkway bare. The facades of the deserted storefronts looked gray and spooky. Others were either boarded up or condemned.

An "out of business" sign hung over the door of a travel agency next to Juliano's. J.C. stopped to look through the dusty, stained window at the colorful travel posters and wondered if he had ever been to the Caribbean, Mexico, or the Virgin Islands. Anywhere would be fine if he could only remember one thing, one lousy incident that might jar his memory. He hoped all those missing memories would come flooding back to light up his life, make it mean something, give him roots.

Wally had been standing next to Juliano's staring at the window displays. "Look at this," he said. "All the furniture was made by Heathwood."

Wally's voice jarred J.C. back to reality. He tried to focus on what Wally had said. "Yeah, so . . ."

"So let's go in," Wally said. "Time's a wastin'."

Wally walked in like a take-charge guy, aggressive, determined, and focused. J.C. had a hard time keeping up with him. The salesman with the bad leg tried to stand up and greet them, but sat down again as Wally whizzed past him to the rear of the store.

Wally stopped at the counter in front of the office. The door was partially open. Troy Butterfield was at his desk. "Mister Butterfield." Wally stood at attention. "I'm Wallace Dunlevy, northeast deputy sales director in charge of publicity."

Troy looked up from what he was doing like a deer staring at headlights. "Wha . . . what? Who did you say—"

"Wallace. Wallace Dunlevy, Mister Butterfield," Wally repeated. "I'm here on a promotion for Heathwood's distributors."

Troy jumped up from behind his desk and scurried out of his office like a freshman lapdog. "How can I help you, Mister Dunlevy?"

"Heathwood is putting out a promotional flyer next month with pictures of selected store owners. We've selected you to be one of them."

Troy looked stunned, as if he couldn't believe what he was hearing. "Sure, sure I ah . . . where do you want—"

Wally waved his arm toward J.C. "This is my photographer, Jack Mulgrew. Where would you like Mister Butterfield, Jack?"

J.C. stepped forward. "Right here, sir," he said pointing to an imaginary spot on the floor. "Mister Dunlevy." He paused to smirk at Wally. "You can stand right here." J.C. pointed to a spot next to Troy.

The two men stood next to each other, Troy displayed a smile of sincere appreciation. Wally's face reflected a facade as empty as the storefronts they had passed when walking to the store.

J.C. snapped the shutter three times capturing the electronic image of what he hoped might be a suspect in the reverend's murder and possibly Jason Saxberg's. "Thanks a lot, sir," he said. "That's all I need."

Wally extended his hand and smiled like a politician. "We'll send this to home office. They'll send it to their printer. Keep up the good work Mister Butterfield, this publicity will help."

Wally walked out as briskly as he came in, J.C. in hot pursuit. They scampered to the truck and drove to Ducheck's where J.C. printed the three 8x10 pictures on his printer.

"What now?" J.C. asked.

Wally looked at the clock above the bar. "One thirty. If we hurry, we can catch the fourth race."

"Fourth race? Where?"

"Wheeling. My friend Earoff doesn't miss Wednesday's dog races. I want to show him a picture of Troy Butterfield."

#

The parking lot was crowded. People going to the Wednesday Dog Races added considerably to the multitude of casino gamblers. Wally and J.C. walked sideways like beach crabs through the thick crowd in the casino to the escalator. One dollar gained them entrance to the second floor and freedom from the crazed gambling mob.

Wally spotted his friend seated at a table near the rail. He had a perfect seat, near the bar and close to the betting windows.

"Earoff," Wally said. "What's shakin'?"

A pudgy, freckle-faced man with shoulder-length auburn hair looked up. "Hey Walt, how's it goin'? What's with the hair? You look like Gladstone Duck." He stretched his flabby, wrinkled arm, gesturing for them to sit down. "Have a seat. What can I do for you?"

Wally smiled, pulled out a chair and signaled for a waitress before sitting down. "This is J.C. Ducheck. He owns Ducheck's Bar. Good friend of mine."

Earoff made a feeble attempt to stand and extended his hand. "Any friend of Walt's."

Loud speakers announced the beginning of the fifth race. A pretty brunette waitress appeared. Wally ordered a round of beers. They waited for the race to end amid shouting and threats from anxious ticket holders until cursing could be heard, signifying the end of the race, and the winner.

"That fat, fuckin' bitch," Earoff said, ripping up his ticket. "You can't trust a woman not even a pudgy, four-legged hairy one." He threw the shards of paper toward the ashtray, missing it "J.C. Ducheck huh? Was John your father?"

"No, but close," J.C. said. "Helped me out when I needed it. Gave me a job bartending and when he died, left the place to me."

"Yeah, now I remember," Earoff said. "You were found up on the Interstate, in a creek, wasn't it? About three years ago?"

"Yeah," J.C. said, lowering his head. "That's me all right. The man that saved my life that day was murdered. We're trying to find out who did it."

Wally took a draw on his beer and looked at Earoff. "Remember you told me about seeing Reverend Smith in Atlantic City."

"Yeah, I remember."

"You said he was dressed up, disguised as a rabbi."

"Remember that too."

"You also said he was in a heated discussion with a younger man, a man with a pointed face that looked like Pee Wee Herman." Wally motioned for J.C. to open the envelope that contained the pictures.

"Yep, I remember that night," Earoff said, looking up in a wistful manner. "I won a bundle."

"Is this the guy," Wally said, placing the pictures on the table.

"That's him all right," Earoff said, thumping his index finger on the digital representation of Troy. "They were having a real spat, for sure."

Wally grabbed the pictures back. "When I talked to you before, you mentioned they were talking about money. Can you be more specific?"

Earoff scratched his head. "Well, they were both mad.

The runt was really mad. He kept saying that he needed the money, that the reverend owed him."

J.C. jumped in. "Anything else? Did he say what the money was for?"

"I took it that the runt was in business," Earoff said. "He kept saying the business was failing and the reverend was late on his payments."

"Payments?" Wally asked. "You're sure he said payments?"

"Yep, payments."

Wally gulped the rest of his beer and left a ten on the table. "Let's go J.C., we've got work to do."

#

The planning and coordination between Paul and the two amateur detectives took place in the back room at Ducheck's.

Wally had just finished telling Paul about their meeting with Earoff when J.C. arrived with a tray of drinks. He slid the bottles of I.C. Light across the table as if he was playing shuffleboard; the double shot of Bellows he placed carefully in front of Paul.

Paul pushed the bourbon back toward J.C. "I won't be needing this."

Wally's face lit up. He looked at J.C. and giggled.

"What do you think Paul?" J.C. asked. He felt Paul had turned the corner, he was coming back to his former self. "Do you think Troy Butterfield was blackmailing the reverend? Do you think he killed him?"

"Can't tell yet." Paul drew on his cigarette. "Maybe it was furniture payments. Could've been anything. Maybe the reverend was paying for sex."

"Can you subpoena Troy's financial records," J.C. asked.

"No, I can't do that," Paul replied, "but I'll find out. Leave it to me."

Chapter 28

Paul noticed the salesman trying to get out of the plush chair in which he was enveloped and waved him off, saving him the time and trouble of a wasted sales attempt. The man recognized Paul, however and was already descending into his upholstered lair, to wait for his next sales prey.

Paul whizzed past to the counter in the back of the store and tapped the plunger on a circular, silver bell. Troy Butterfield sat at his desk, looking through a stack of papers, probably bills from the look on his face. He glanced up and dropped the load on his desk as if he was throwing out the garbage.

"Detective," Troy said feebly, as if he didn't want to be bothered. "What is it you want this time?"

"Do you have one of those lift chairs I see advertised on television?"

Troy stood up and darted for the counter. "I have one in the back. If—"

"Not for me," Paul said. "For your salesman. He has a hard time climbing out of that 'Lazy Boy'."

Troy's shoulders slumped. "What do you want Detective?"

"I want to know more about your relationship with Reverend Smith."

Troy motioned to his salesman. "Harry, you can take your lunch now." They watched Harry fight his way out of the chair lumber out of the store. Troy continued. "I told you everything the other day. What more—"

"Do you know Earoff Matta?" Paul asked.

"Hell no," Troy said, his face screwing up as if he had just sucked a lemon. "Earoff. What kind of name is that? What kind of person—"

"The kind that goes to Atlantic City and gambles. He said he saw you there with Reverend Smith."

Troy fidgeted with a pencil and started writing something in an appointment book. "Why would I be with Reverend Smith after what I told you the other day?"

Paul scratched his head and then looked straight into Troy's eyes. "Blackmail comes to mind."

Troy's eyes widened, a look of bewilderment covered his face. "I . . . I don't know what you mean."

"Earoff overheard a heated argument you had with the reverend about money. Do you remember now or shall I ask you again in court?"

"The son of a bitch was late on a payment." Troy said, visibly shaken, his arms flailing. "He was gambling and showing his boyfriend a good time with my money. Why wouldn't I get mad?"

"What do you mean your money?"

"I found out about the arrangement my father had with the reverend. I didn't say anything about it until after my father got sick with Alzheimers. I told the reverend that the payment was to be continued, paid to me." He looked at Paul, the look of pleading escaped from his eyes. "The business was in a slump and besides, I was the one who was violated, not my father. I needed that money. Why not get it from that hypocritical son of a bitch who ruined my life? Who better?"

"How much was he paying you?"

Troy hesitated as if he had already said too much. "Three hundred dollars a month. That's nothing compared to the misery that mother-fucker caused me. I used it for the business anyway, it's not like I really enjoyed it." Troy spread his hands on the counter and seemed to calm down. "By the way, I won't admit to anything in court that we just talked about."

"I understand that you don't want this publicized, but I have a murder to solve and you have motive."

"What motive? I didn't have any reason to kill him. He was late on a payment sure, but he always paid. I needed the money. Why would I kill him?"

"You hated him, didn't you?"

"I did, but I didn't kill him. I wouldn't kill anyone."

"Where were you the day the reverend was murdered?"

"Right here at the store. We started early that day with monthly inventory. Ask Harry, he helped me."

"I will. Where were you the night Jason Saxberg was murdered?"

"What? Do you think I had anything to do with Jason's murder? You're crazy. What the hell do you think I am? Sure, I was abused by the reverend, but I don't go around taking it out on others by killing them."

"Do you remember where you were that night?"

Troy looked at Paul with a deadpan expression. "The same place I am every night; upstairs, taking care of my dad. Why would you ask me about Jason's murder? We were friends."

"You were on the rifle team, right?"

"Well . . . yeah, but so what?"

"What do you know about Fleming?"

"I heard he's a pusher—big time."

Paul hesitated, then asked, "What about Hawkins? Was he into drugs too?"

"Yeah, I heard Hawkins was trying to make the big leagues and tried to muscle in on Fleming's territory."

"Where'd you hear this information?"

"From my customers. They talk a lot." Troy's eyes widened. "I just remembered something when you mentioned Fleming and Hawkins in context with the reverend."

Paul leaned closer. This might be what he was waiting for, a new direction that might speed up the case.

"I remember that Hawkins confronted Fleming one day on the range. Something about Fleming working for the reverend."

"Is that all?" Paul asked.

"I couldn't make out what they were saying, but it seemed Hawkins knew something about Fleming and the reverend."

"But you don't know what?"

"No, but I got a clear impression that the reverend and Fleming had a close connection, and Hawkins knew about it."

Paul sat back and took notes. "What kind of vehicle do you drive?"

"A Chevy Cavalier. Why?"

"Does your father have a vehicle?"

"Sold it."

Paul excused himself and left.

#

"No, I don't believe Troy Butterfield had anything to do with the reverend's murder," Paul said, taking a sip from the frosted mug. "He didn't have motive."

"Money is a motive," Wally said.

"Money is a very good motive, but in this case, Troy would be eliminating his money source by killing the reverend."

"Can't you press charges against Troy for blackmail?" J.C. asked.

"Wouldn't be worth it," Paul said, dragging on his cigarette. "It would be hard to prove. Troy runs a business. He could say the three hundred dollars a month was furniture payments or the reverend was paying back a debt. No one could refute it; the reverend's dead. Hell, for all I know, the reverend could have paid Troy in cash."

"What about Jason's murder?" J.C. asked. "Could Troy be involved?"

"I had his alibi's checked out, he's clean," Paul motioned toward J.C. "The night someone tried to kill you, Troy was in the emergency room with his father. And he doesn't drive a dark truck. He has a Chevy Cavalier."

"Looks like a dead end," Wally said.

"Hold the phone," Paul said. "I did get some information out of Troy. He said that Hawkins knew about a connection between the reverend and Fleming."

"We have to find Hawkins then." Wally said.

"You guys were in Hawkins' house. Can you remember anything that might tell us where he went?"

Wally squinted his eyes and looked off into the distance as if he was trying to remember something.

J.C. was thinking about what Paul had just said, about the connection between the reverend and Fleming. "There was a picture of the rifle team on the wall, remember Wally? I didn't recognize him at first, but Troy Butterfield was the rat-faced boy in the picture."

"Yeah, so what?" Wally asked. "That's why he knows about the reverend and his connections."

"How does that in any way tell us where Hawkins is?" Paul asked.

J.C. sat upright in his chair. "When you were talking about the connections between Fleming and Hawkins, it was just a question, but when you talked about Butterfield, the picture on the wall in Hawkins' office popped into my head."

"It's just a picture of the rifle team." Wally said.

"You're right Wally," J.C. said, "but where was it taken?"

Wally had a dumbfounded look on his face. "Why would it matter?"

"It might matter a lot," Paul said. He quickly pulled out his notepad. "Where was it taken?"

"There was a sign in the background," J.C. said. "Camp Perry was the name of the place where the picture was taken."

Wally slumped back into his seat. "So. How can that help us? They could have shot at a lot of ranges."

Paul was writing on his notepad. "This could be very helpful. Camp Perry has annual competitions."

"So," Wally said, his palms upturned.

Paul smiled. "The competitions are next week. If he loves shooting as much as you say he does, he'll be there. He might go Tuesday for the individual practice session before the competitions start."

"Absolutely," J.C. said. "He's on the run. He has to go somewhere."

Chapter 29

Eleven days had passed since Paul had requested information on Mark Smith. As soon as he arrived at his desk Monday morning, he picked up the phone and dialed the Fayetteville, North Carolina, Police Department. The dispatcher forwarded his call to Sergeant Thornton.

"Andrews, I was about to call you," he said in a voice that wrought of insincerity. "I have some dates for you."

"Good. They'll be important," Paul said, feeling his blood pressure rising. He knew they had taken their time checking on Mark's whereabouts. "Wha'da'ya' got?"

"Okay. In chronological order. Mark Smith was not in town on July the third."

"Okay," Paul marked an "X" in his notebook next to the day that Jason Saxberg was murdered. "What's next?"

"July the ninth."

Paul scratched another "X" next to the day Reverend Smith was murdered. He felt anxious. "Was he in town?"

"Yes, he was in town on the ninth, but out of town on the fifteenth."

"What about the nineteenth and the twenty third?"

"He was in town on those dates," Thornton said.

Paul's heart sank. He marked X's next to the days of Fleming's murder and the attempt on Wally and J.C. He felt let down that the dates that Mark was out of town didn't include the date the reverend was murdered. There had to be two murderers, either completely separate or Mark had an accomplice.

"Can you confirm those dates?"

"I had patrolmen canvass the neighbors, the restaurant where he had lunch every day, even the hippy bookstore where he spent most of his time."

"Was there someone in his apartment complex that saw him every day, someone who could vouch for his whereabouts?"

"He did have a roommate, but he moved out about a month ago."

"A roommate? Do you have his name?"

Paul could hear papers being shuffled.

"No, I don't have his name."

"Look," Paul said. "This could be important. Can you get me his roommate's name, description and any background information you have on him?"

"Well . . . it might take a few—"

"Sarge, I don't have a few more days. Two people may be in danger. I need it now."

"That important, huh?"

"That important."

"I'll check on it right now, Detective. I'll get back to you as soon as I can."

#

Paul walked with a swagger, like a man who knew he was going to be off for nine days. Saturday and Sunday plus a week's vacation and the next weekend as well. The time off would provide a much-needed rest from the job, plus give him the opportunity to go with Wally and J.C. to Camp Perry. He walked past the Customer Service Counter, a misnomer for a place where felons of all types got acquainted with the desk sergeant.

A young man with a bewildered look on his face sat handcuffed on the left side of the room. He had long, black hair and was wearing a black trench coat, odd for the summer season; probably a shoplifter. A balding, middle-aged man was arguing with a uniformed officer. He was close to getting in the officer's face, his closing purple eye looked pathetic next to the other defiant, brown one. A young girl with short, green hair sat on a bench opposite the gothic pilferer, her micro-mini skirt revealing shapely thighs. She smiled at Paul, one of those gestures of either desperation or pure habit from years of being on the street.

Paul glided through the noisy menagerie toward the rear elevator. He got off on the second floor and strode down the marble hallway toward Captain Henderson's office.

The captain's door was open; Paul walked in. The look on the captain's face drained away any feeling of exhilaration Paul might have had—one of those looks you see at funeral homes.

"Paul, I'm sorry but your vacation request was denied."

"What? I don't understand. I haven't had time off for seven months, I have three weeks coming."

The captain lowered his head, shuffled through some papers picking one out. "I okayed it Paul; it was stopped upstairs."

"What the hell for? What—"

The captain interrupted by reading from the sheet he had plucked from the pile. "Due to a shortage of manpower and the timeliness of the request, Detective Andrew's petition for vacation is denied."

"I need that time, captain. What about a couple'a personal days?"

"I already tried it. The commander was steadfast in his

decision. I always try to oblige my men. You know that Paul. What's so important that you need this time?"

Paul explained the situation about Hawkins and that he might be at the shooting range in Camp Perry.

"I'll notify the Port Clinton police and have them—"

"Won't work, captain. He's on the lam and street smart. He'll be using a fictitious name and he would have changed plates by now. And we don't have any photos of him to forward."

Captain Henderson put the request form back in the stack of papers. "Sorry Paul. I wish I could help. What about next week? Will he be gone?"

"Like the wind. Like the fuckin' disappearing wind," Paul aid as he left the office.

#

Paul had just finished telling J.C. and Wally about the meeting with Captain Henderson. "Nuggets, bring another round," he said, not finishing the bottle in front of him.

"That's pretty shitty," Wally said. "The captain not granting your vacation request."

Paul waved a negative arm at Wally's statement. "The captain's a stand-up guy. He signed my request. Third floor put the kybosh on it."

"Why?" J.C. asked.

"Said I didn't put in for it in time, said that they were short on manpower. We are a little short on manpower, but that never stopped a vacation in the past."

Wally rubbed his chin. "Maybe the commander's bucking for chief."

"Could be," Paul said, "but that isn't helping the case now. Is it?"

"Why don't J.C. and I go?" Wally asked.

J.C. figured Wally would ask and was preparing a logical statement in his mind. "Yeah, we could surveil the shooting range for Hawkins and follow him to where he's staying. We'll question him. If he won't talk, we'll call the Port Clinton Police."

What J.C. and Wally had proposed made sense, but Paul had reservations. They weren't cops; they wouldn't know how to follow Hawkins properly. What if they screwed up? What if Hawkins could be a danger to them? What if the person looking for Hawkins was the killer? What was the alternative? The Port Clinton Poice couldn't do it. They wouldn't know who to look for and they certainly wouldn't assign an officer to go with them.

He considered Wally and J.C.'s request carefully, noting that Wally needed to feel of important and that J.C. desperately had to find his identity.

Paul's decision was made. "Sounds like a plan. I'll fill them in on what you're doing and to expect your call."

Wally and J.C. looked at each other, surprised.

"What?" Paul's eyebrows arched high on his forehead and his palms opened in a defensive manner. "I was going to have you two tag along anyway."

"We'll leave tomorrow morning then," Wally said. "We'll get there when the shooting range opens. We'll find a place to stay later."

"I have a friend who has a connection in the Port Clinton area," Paul said. "You'll be staying at the Holiday Inn at Catawba Island."

"I'm impressed," Wally said. "You have connections all over, don't you?"

Paul grinned. "I have a few friends."

Chapter 30

Wally's truck rumbled across the Glenfield Bridge on I-79 North. He had another sixty-three miles to Ohio; J.C. would take over then. But first, a brief stop in Warrendale for breakfast, only ten minutes away.

J.C. gazed at the rolling hills, forests, and patchwork farmland that made up Pennsylvania's landscape, thinking over the details that Paul had gone over with them. Paul was very logical and J.C. wouldn't hesitate to follow his directions. Because they had left at 5 a.m., it made sense to check into the hotel first. There would be plenty of time to register and make it to Camp Perry in time for the practice round or a quick snooze and a shower.

Paul's concerns about Hawkins worried J.C. He wasn't afraid of Hawkins if it came to a confrontation or a fight. Rather it was something Paul had said about someone else being after Hawkins. Paul didn't want J.C. or Wally to get in the middle.

J.C. remembered how Paul looked when he barked out his orders about keeping distant. J.C. felt very uneasy and wondered if trouble was around the corner. He felt a chill down his back, as he had earlier, but knew this trip was the only way to find Jason's murderer, to help solve the mystery of his identity and make a life with Barb possible.

"Just follow Hawkins to where he's staying," Paul had said, "Call the police, they'll take it from there."

J.C. wondered if Hawkins would talk to the police. Criminals, he thought, follow the code of silence. They don't talk; they clam up. Maybe we can find a better way. I'll convince Wally; that's what I'll do.

"Look like you're thinking about something," Wally said. "What's on your mind?"

"Bring your binoculars?"

"In my overnight bag. Couldn't forget 'em, they were on my nightstand."

"On your nightstand?" Why do you keep spy-glasses on your nightstand?"

"Ah . . . no reason," Wally looked away.

"Couldn't be that new neighbor, could it? The young divorcée . . . what's her name?"

"Toni—I mean Antoinette. Antoinette Pallini. And she's not the reason I have my glasses on my nightstand," Wally said. "I watch my pigeons."

"The pigeons are in your back yard, aren't they?"

"Well, I have a few retarded ones." Wally couldn't hold back a grin, but quickly got serious. "There's Perkins. Let's eat."

#

After they left the restaurant, Wally continued driving for another fifty-three miles to exit 60, burping up the taste of sausage gravy and bacon as he drove. J.C. then took over. After another four routes and twenty-five minutes, they arrived at Catawba Island.

The sign read, Holiday Inn Express Hotel and Suites, Port Clinton. The main lobby, lounge chairs and tables, was awash with pastel colors. The carpeting was a vivid, multi-colored print on a black background.

Their spacious suite was decorated with wildlife photos and vases filled with brightly colored flowers.

"How many days did Paul's friend say we could stay here?"

"Two nights," Wally said. "Then we have to leave or pay for the room."

"What time is it?"

"Ten-thirty. Why?"

"I have time to go to the pool. It looks inviting."

"Can you swim?"

"Maybe I'll take a nap instead," J.C. said, not knowing if he could swim. "I'm tired. What time are you setting the alarm for?"

Wally grabbed the clock and fumbled with the buttons. "Eleven-thirty. That'll give us time to eat and make the rifle range before two o'clock."

#

Six miles separated the hotel from Port Clinton. J.C. had been listening to Wally act as a tour guide. He talked about the annual Walleye Festival in May that attracted fishermen for hundreds of miles.

"Every year a Walleye Princess is crowned for the occasion."

J.C. turned the volume up slightly on the radio. "That must have been exciting."

"One year a bunch of drunken anglers from Donora stuffed the ballot box."

J.C. looked puzzled. "So?"

"Does the name Dominick Angelo ring a bell?"

"I don't hear any bells."

"He's gay," Wally said, laughing. "He went along with the gag and wore a shoulder-length wig and pink-painted waders when he accepted the crown."

J.C. thought it nice that Angelo went along with his friends' gag but wondered about their motives. The fact that they were friends bothered him.

They were bypassing Port Clinton on Route 163; it would be another seven miles to Camp Perry. J.C. didn't know how much more of Wally's tour guide speech he could take. Wally continued driving on 163, called Lake Shore Drive, until he got off on Route 358. There was a railroad spur running parallel to the road. To the left was an airplane landing strip. A mile drive ended at the shooting range. They drove past refurbished World War II barracks and other assorted army-type buildings that were painted pastel peach with chocolate brown roofs. It was two o'clock.

"Look at all the people," J.C. said. "I didn't know there were so many shooters."

All the participants, their friends and family members crowded the edge of the firing line, reflecting a kaleidoscope of colors from various styles of shooting apparel. Buttons and patches that represented past accomplishments were displayed on baseball caps. Some caps had side shields on their beaks to keep out sunlight. A standard shooting outfit evidently wasn't required, J.C. thought, even his blue double-pocketed shirt and gray slacks would qualify his presence on the firing line.

"Actually there are more," Wally said. "This time allotment is for individual practice. They're fifth priority. The teams have already practiced and qualified."

"Since it's a low priority, Hawkins probably wouldn't need reservations?" J.C. asked.

"That's right. He'd just be another face in the crowd."

Modified canvas shopping carts, fold-up seats, ingenious shooting stands, spotting scopes and fancy ultra modern rifles were placed around each shooter's position. The shooters wore protective Mickey-Mouse ears and tinted shooting glasses.

Wally and J.C. picked a spot next to a concession stand from which they could scan the shooting range. They were far enough away that they didn't need ear protection and could still view the entire field.

Wally was already checking out the field. "I can't see. It's too level here," he said. "I need to get higher."

J.C. pointed to a set of shiny aluminum framed bleachers ten tiers high. "Let's go over there."

They climbed to the top, sat down and rested their backs on the warm metal railings. Wally grabbed his binoculars and looked over the firing line.

J.C. gazed at the huge crowd on the range and wondered why so many people were interested in shooting rifles. Were they hunters, or ex-servicemen? Maybe they were members of the militia he had read about or drug dealers, like Hawkins. He thought they could be using their time more effectively, instead of poking holes in paper with high-powered projectiles. And women? Why on earth would women be firing rifles? Was it part of the women's lib thing he had heard about, or the *I can do anything a man can do, and maybe better routine* he had heard young girls banter after a few beers. In any case, he was nervous. He didn't like being around people with guns; he'd rather be around drunks.

"I think I see him," Wally said, rising up in his seat like a groundhog who hears a whistle. "Take a look." He pointed to an area on the firing line, near the center.

"Where?" J.C. asked. ""Near that fat guy in the red shirt?"

"To the right. About eight or nine people."

"In a dark gray and white shooting coat?"

Wally grunted his agreement.

Hawkins' shooting coat covered a blue shirt and beige chaps sheltered white trousers. He wore a multi-colored baseball cap; the skull section was red with white side panels. The blue beak had fold-down sides to keep out the sunlight. He had red mouse-ear protection strapped around his head, and amber-colored shooting glasses covered his eyes. He was shooting a thick-barreled, fancy rifle from a distance of six hundred yards.

#

Wally and J.C. waited two hours until J.C.'s impatience got the best of him. He wanted to search the parking lot for the Bravada to avoid losing Hawkins in the crowd.

"There could be a dozen vehicles of that style," Wally said, "and what if he left early? I'd have to hunt for you."

So they waited. Finally, at four o'clock, Hawkins started to pack up his gear. Lucky for Wally and J.C. only a few people were leaving. The black Bravada pulled out of its parking stall and headed out of the compound, past the orderly barracks and the airfield onto Lake Shore Drive.

Between Camp Perry and Port Clinton, Route 163 crosses an isthmus. While only one and three-quarter miles long, the isthmus provided a scenic view of both the inlet and the lake. Hawkins drove over the bridge and hung a left, staying on Route 163. Wally followed at a safe distance. Hawkins continued east for fourteen blocks, then turned right. Wally made the turn, being careful to stay far back enough to keep from being made. He saw Hawkins making a left turn three blocks ahead.

"Step on it, Wally. We're losing him."

Wally floored it. The truck leaped forward "We'll catch him. I didn't come this far—"

"Wally! Watch out!" J.C. said, bracing his arms against the dash.

A white soccer ball had bounced out onto the street from the rear of a parked car. Wally hit the brakes and screeched to a swerving stop. A dark green truck that had been in back of them also screeched to a stop. Wally looked in the rear-view mirror to signal an apology, but couldn't see the driver through the truck's tinted windshield. He couldn't wait; he had to follow Hawkins. A wide-eyed little boy appeared between the cars and waited for Wally to signal him to get the ball. The little boy scurried to retrieve it, and then disappeared into the greenness of his yard.

Wally wiped his forehead and restarted the engine, which had stalled because of the sudden stop. "Holy shit," he said, stepping on the gas. He headed for the intersection where he last saw Hawkins turn left. No one in sight.

"Damn it," Wally said. "We lost him."

"Let's try to catch up. He can't be too far ahead."

Wally sped down East State Street, but the black Bravada had disappeared. J.C. thought Hawkins had made a clean get-away. What would they tell Paul, that they lost him in practically no traffic in a small town in a residential neighborhood? J.C. didn't want to believe that they came this close and failed. It isn't fair, he thought, why would this happen? How would they ever bring Jason's murderer to justice? J.C. was shaking his head from side to side in disgust when he noticed the black SUV, off to the left in the rear of a gray stone building. Hawkins was walking into the building.

"Keep going!" J.C. said. "Don't slow down!"

"Why? What's the matter?"

J.C. looked straight ahead. "It's Hawkins," he said, pointing to a road to the right that led across the railroad tracks. "Pull in here."

Wally swung the Chevy onto a dusty access road and came to a stop. "What do you mean its Hawkins?"

"He's back there," J.C. said turning around in his seat and gesturing toward the direction they had come.

Wally turned the truck around and headed back.

"He walked into that gray building." J.C. thought the building was probably an auto parts store at first, but now noticed a sign in front of it. "Granny's Home Cook'n" he said. "That's where he is."

Chapter 31

Paul walked in Ducheck's armed with information he had received earlier that morning from Sergeant Thornton. Business had picked up, Paul thought. It was only 9:30 a.m. and three men were huddled at the near end of the bar, drinking shots and washing them down with drafts. Nuggets was at the other end of the bar on the phone. He hung up when he saw Paul come in and started walking toward him.

"Didn't think you were off duty today," Nuggets said. "What'll you have?"

Paul held up his hand then pointed his finger toward the empty seats at the far end of the bar. Paul sat on a stool next to the opening that led to the back room. Nuggets joined him.

"Know my schedule, do you? What else do you make it your business to know?"

Nuggets seemed to stop breathing. There was a look of disbelief on his face. After a few seconds, his eyes glanced around the room as if seeking an answer. He stuttered, "I, I don't . . ." He forced a crooked smile and recovered. "What do you mean Paul?"

"I was talking to Sergeant Thornton of the Fayetteville, North Carolina, Police Department," Paul said, watching what was left of Nuggets' energy drain from his face. "Funny thing. Your description matches that of Mark Smith's roommate."

Nuggets started to open his mouth to protest, but before he could, Paul said, "The same roommate who left Fayetteville a few days before you showed up here."

Nuggets looked to his left, toward the opening that led to the back room and eventually to the rear door.

"Don't try it. I've got patrolmen outside. It'll get ugly."

Paul didn't want to get physical with Nuggets or chase him down the street, so he was lying about the officers being outside. Luckily, Nuggets believed him. He slumped against the bar in resignation.

Paul walked behind the bar. "Assume the position," he said, reaching for his cuffs.

Nuggets spread his legs and leaned on the bar with outstretched arms. Paul placed the handcuffs securely on Nuggets' wrists before patting him down.

The three men at the end of the bar started to get up. Paul flashed his tin. "Bar's closed."

One of the men reached for his beer.

"Now," Paul said, grabbing Nuggets by the arm and leading him to a table near the bar. He locked the door after the three men left.

"Now, let's go over the setup you had with Mark Smith." Paul sat across the table from Nuggets. He refrained from calling him Nuggets as that would imply that he hadn't received confirmation of his identity or his relationship with Mark Smith. By saying *let's go over the setup*, Paul intimated that he knew about the relationship with Mark—but that's a cop's trick.

"I don't have any deal with Mark," Nuggets said.

"Yeah, right. You just left Fayetteville to come up here and tend bar for minimum wage. You think I'm stupid? Come clean. The more you cooperate, the easier it will be for you."

"Easier? Easier for what? Nebshitting? That's all I did, relay information."

"We're talking about three murder cases and two attempted murders, *pal.* The relaying of messages or other overt actions make you an accomplice. Maybe you're shittin' me and you actually committed a murder or an attempted murder or two. Then it's the gas chamber for you."

Nuggets' attitude changed; he looked scared—really scared. "I didn't hurt anyone. I didn't attempt to hurt anyone. All I did was give Mark information."

"Why would you do that? Out of the goodness of your heart? Come on. What do you take me for . . . a fool?"

"Mark promised me something lucrative. Something I couldn't pass up."

"What would that be?"

"Something I did before—somewhere else. I can't say. I don't want to incriminate myself."

Paul figured he was at the end of his questioning, Nuggets was starting to get legal. "Okay, let's go."

Nuggets stood up. "Where are we going?"

"Downtown."

"You're arresting me? What's the charge?"

"Nebshitting. Now let's go," Paul knew he could detain Nuggets for only so long but he wanted to question him later, after he thought about it for a while. He'd come up with a charge to hold him until then.

Paul knew that the murders of the reverend and Fleming and the attempted murder of Wally and J.C. coincided with times when Mark was in Fayetteville. He wondered if Nuggets was the perpetrator or if he was giving information to someone else—maybe Mark's accomplice. Maybe a completely separate murderer existed.

#

Wally and J.C. had to find a location to watch the restaurant. They had to tail Hawkins until they found where he was staying and then call the Port Clinton Police,

"Pull in here," J.C. said, pointing to the only side street between their turnaround and the restaurant.

Wally turned right and then a quick left. They were in view of Granny's now, a perfect position providing access to other roads leading from the restaurant.

While Wally and J.C. were sitting in the truck, they tried not to look suspicious. Wally had spread a roadmap over the dashboard in plain sight, pretending they were lost travelers.

They waited for one hour. It was 5:45 p.m. when J.C. jostled Wally's shoulder.

"Wally, it's him," J.C. said, pointing toward Granny's.

Hawkins' pulled out of the parking lot and headed east. Wally started the truck and waited for Hawkins to pass the intersection before tailing him. Good thing he waited. Hawkins slowed down and started to turn toward them.

"He's heading for us," J.C. said, slouching down in his seat.

"Oh shit," Wally picked up the map to cover their faces as Hawkins sped past.

Hawkins headed northeast, along the shoreline of Lake Erie. Two and a half miles later, Hawkins pulled into the parking lot of the Scenic Rock Ledge Inn. Five cabins were in the rear, nestled among the trees that bordered the property. The main lodge, which was perched on a knoll a mere twenty yards from the road, provided a scenic view of the lake.

The main inn resembled a barn. The huge, three-storey aqua colored building, with dormers on the third floor, stuck out in contrast with the surrounding forest. The spacious front porch supported a dozen rocking chairs. American flags hung over the railings. Wally slowly drove past the inn trying to spot Hawkins. Hawkins drove through the main parking lot and headed for the cabins.

There were five cabins in the rear. He pulled into the driveway of the fourth cabin, a small, red brick with white trim. A small redwood deck protruded from the right side of the front porch.

Once they were sure where Hawkins was, Wally continued down the road for a short distance. They were surprised when they came to the intersection of NW Catawba Road.

"Look at that," J.C. said, pointing to a promotional sign for the Holiday Inn Express Hotel. "One mile to our hotel."

"Well, at least we know where we are. Now what are we going to do?"

J.C. knew Wally wanted to call the Port Clinton Police. "Let's talk to Hawkins first, then call the police. What do you think?"

"I think we should call the police now."

J.C. hesitated. "I don't know . . . calling in the police might make him clam up. We could screw things up."

Wally pulled out his cell phone and punched in Paul's number. "Let's ask Paul."

Chapter 32

The trip to Port Clinton involved more than Wally and J.C. had bargained for. Back in the city, Paul had just finished talking to Sergeant Thornton of the Fayetteville, North Carolina, Police Department. Thornton said Mark's apartment was empty, cleaned out. He'd left town; nobody knew when or where he went.

The phone rang. Paul picked up on the third ring.

"Paul? Wally. We've located—"

"Wally, I've been trying to reach you. I called the hotel. You didn't give me your cell phone number."

"I forgot, I didn't think you needed it."

"I just got some information on Mark Smith. I think he's involved in Jason's murder."

"Really, that's great. What do you have?"

"No time to explain. Look, Mark's not in Fayetteville and he's not around here. He may be after Hawkins. Be careful. In fact, you'd better beat a path back home."

On the other end of the line, Wally stared off at the lake. He was concerned Mark might be in the area and possibly after them as well. "Paul we've found Hawkins, he's—"

"You're breaking up."

"What's that Paul?" Wally shouted. "You're breaking up. I can't hear you." Wally shook the cell phone. "All I hear is static." The phone's display showed that the battery was at its lowest level. "Shit, the battery's dead."

"What did Paul say?" J.C. asked.

Wally told J.C. what Paul suspected and that Mark might be in the area.

"We'd better talk to Hawkins. We can't call the police and Mark might get to him before we do."

Wally knew J.C. was right. He turned the truck around and headed back towards the Scenic Rock Ledge Inn. Hawkins' Bravada came toward them, heading north.

Wally covered his forehead with his left hand as if he was wiping sweat from his brow. J.C. quickly picked up a map, peering over the top at Hawkins' truck.

"Do you think he saw us?" Wally asked.

"No he was looking straight ahead."

A dark green truck sped past them, following Hawkins. J.C. looked puzzled. "That dark green truck looks like the one that almost rear-ended us when we were following Hawkins to Granny's."

Wally looked for a place to turn around. "So?"

"So? It also looks like the one that tried to run me off the road that night when I was coming back from the community college."

Wally braked and turned the truck to the left, crossing the northbound lane, plowing into shrubbery and saplings along the east berm of the road. He jammed the gearshift into reverse and peeled wheels as the truck lurched back onto the highway, facing north. The truck hadn't stopped when Wally shifted into first gear. He tramped on the accelerator and laid rubber.

The dark green truck pulled alongside the Bravada. Blue smoke appeared from Hawkins' SUV as it swerved recklessly back and forth across the oncoming lane of traffic. It finally came to a stop; the truck sped away.

Wally pulled off the road in back of the Bravada. The engine was still running. Hawkins was slumped over the steering wheel.

Wally reached the driver's door first. "Ben, Ben Hawkins," he said, watching the blood spurt from Hawkins neck.

J.C. retrieved a plastic sandwich bag from the dashboard of the truck. He pushed Wally aside and clamped it over the wound with his right hand to stop the bleeding. He used his left hand to pull Hawkins' body to an upright position. "Hawkins. Can you hear me? Who shot you?"

His eyes fluttered. J.C. thought he was regaining consciousness. He knew he had to be quick; the wound looked like it might be fatal.

"The man who shot you, was it Jason's boyfriend?" J.C. searched the man's eyes for an affirmative response.

Hawkins' lips started to quiver. "The commander's . . . ." He drifted off.

"The commander?" J.C. jostled Hawkins. "Who? Who was the boyfriend? Who was the boyfriend?"

Hawkins murmured a barely audible, "Tony." He reached for his shirt pocket and tapped it. "Take . . . ." His voice trailed off.

With his left hand J.C. took a folded paper out of Hawkins' pocket. He jammed it into his own shirt pocket, trying not to waste any valuable time, time he needed for answers.

"Tony is the commander's son," Wally said. "That's who he's talking about."

Hawkins slumped over. J.C. took his pulse. "He's dead." He hadn't seen anyone dead before, but somehow knew that he had. J.C. dropped the bloody plastic bag and reached for his handkerchief with his clean hand. He managed to wipe off most of the blood off his right hand.

Wally threw his cell phone in his truck. "We can't call the police."

J.C. walked toward the truck. "If we can't have them come to us . . ."

"Then we'll go to them," Wally finished.

They jumped into the truck, turned around, and headed south. They were approaching the Scenic Rock Lodge when the dark green truck flew up behind them.

"Oh shit!" Wally said.

J.C. turned around in time to see the same truck that had passed before. The tinted windshield obstructed the view of the driver, but he noticed that an open passenger side window was down. The hair on his neck stood up. He had a feeling that the driver was going to shoot at them as he had that night coming home from the community college. The truck was pulling alongside when J.C. stretched over with his foot and tramped on Wally's accelerator foot, lurching them forward.

It was perfect timing. The bullet missed Wally by inches, blasting a hole in the doorframe behind his head. The missile continued past J.C., shattering the small vent window to his right.

Wally kicked J.C.'s foot away. "I'll take it from here," he said flooring the accelerator. "You could've gotten us killed, pulling a stunt like that."

"You're welcome," J.C. said. "I didn't think you needed another hole in your head."

As much as Wally took good care of the old Chevy, it was no match for the newer, black vehicle. The engine sounded supercharged. On a straightaway, the dark green truck pulled alongside them, but instead of the driver shooting at them, he veered the truck to the right, crashing into their front end, forcing them off the road. The area between the road and the lake was covered with large stones, probably put there to keep the shoreline from eroding.

"Wally! Watch out," J.C. yelled as they headed for the boulders.

"I can't—" Wally didn't finish. They hit a large stone and the truck bounced into the air.

The outdated seatbelts in Wally's old chugger were

minimal protection against the jouncing they were taking, forcing J.C. to use his arms to brace himself against the dashboard, but it didn't keep him from moving side-to-side. His head and shoulder kept banging against the window. To protect himself from being knocked out, he folded his right arm around his head. The bouncing motion was crushing them. The sound of metal banged off the rocks, jarring their teeth. They kept ricocheting down the hillside until they hit a larger boulder that sent the truck airborne.

"Whoa!" Wally shouted, as if he was riding a horse, but the sound he made was one of fright. The truck belly-flopped on all fours, creating an enormous splash that radiated billowing waves.

"Wally, you okay?" J.C. was looking out the passenger window into the lake, wondering how they got there; it had happened so fast. *Did I lose my memory again? Is this the way it happened before? No. I know who Wally is.* Then he thought of Barb and remembered what his mission was. *I'm okay.* "Wally?"

"Yeah? I'm not goin' anywhere. Not right now anyway. Get out of your seatbelt."

J.C. frantically jabbed at the release button on the seatbelt, opening it after a few tries. He felt the water gushing in on his feet. He saw the water rising on the floor and spurting in from under the dash. He looked over at Wally and saw water streaming through the bullet hole on the doorframe. In his current incarnation, he didn't know how to swim and terror was beginning to grip him. He reached for the door.

"Hold on there, pardner," Wally said, grabbing J.C.'s arm. "Relax, we'll get out of this. Don't panic."

"But we're sinking," J.C.'s voice rose an octave.

Wally pulled harder on J.C.'s arm. "We have to wait until the water pressure equalizes before we try to get out. The doors won't open before then."

"What if we broke a window?"

"The water pressure would push you back in," Wally said. Most of the truck was submerged now, except for the area above the window. Wally pointed through the windshield. "There's another reason."

J.C. looked through the dispersing water on the windshield to where Wally was pointing. He could make out the silhouette of a man standing on the berm of the road.

J.C. looked frightened. "Oh shit! What do we do now?"

Wally reached under the seat and grabbed a handful of rags, throwing them to J.C. He pointed to the water coming in the damaged vent window. "Here, plug up that hole."

Wally plugged up the bullet hole in his doorframe.

"This won't help," J.C. said, frantically trying to stuff rags at the rushing water. "We're sinking."

The truck was almost fully submerged. Wally talked in a slow, deliberate tone. "We'll get out of this. Trust me."

"But—"

"No buts." Wally said, pointing through the windshield. "We're under water now, but we have enough air to survive for a while."

J.C. settled down, calmed by Wally's voice and a sincere belief that they would get through this, but he had reservations. He pointed toward the floor. "Water's coming in. It's up to my knees already."

"We have to wait until the cab fills up with water to get out." Wally said. "The longer it takes the better, then—"

"The longer it takes? How can that be better?"

"The guy that's waiting on the road can't stick around forever. Either he'll think we're dead or leave when another car comes along. Our chances are better if we wait."

"What if he's still there when we get out of here?" J.C. asked. "What do we do then?"

"Tread water. I don't know, but we wait."

They hadn't sunk very deep yet; J.C. estimated it to be about ten feet. Water was slowly rising in the cab; it was up to their waists now.

"This old heap held together better than I thought it would," Wally said, "I would've thought it would sink like a rock."

"Better for us it didn't, huh?"

They sat and waited for the water to rise. J.C. was extremely nervous but trusted Wally implicitly. The water was now at chest level.

"When the water is at your neck," Wally said, "sit up in your seat and crook your head so you can breathe the last few inches of air."

"Then what?'

"When it's time I'll tell you. You'll open your door and get out. I'll follow you. I'll make sure you get out okay."

J.C. shifted in his seat. "Sounds like a plan."

They sat waiting for the water to rise. Wally looked calm. J.C. wasn't. Finally the water reached the level of J.C.'s neck. He followed Wally's instructions and positioned himself so he could breathe the last few inches of air.

Wally stretched his neck for the remaining gulps of air as well and said, "Okay, J.C., let's go. Open the door."

J.C. took a last big breath, pulled the handle and thrust his weight against the door, slowly pushing it open. He crawled out of the doorway. Wally started to follow, but as he slid across the seat, his foot caught between the floor-shift and the seat. He was wearing his comfortable boots but they were large and bulky. He pulled and yanked on his foot. It wouldn't release. He tried to untie the laces, but the rawhide strings were slippery. When he finally untied them enough to pull his foot partially free, he ran out of breath and passed out.

J.C. broke the surface of the water and gulped in a mouthful of air. He noticed the man on the road was gone. He suddenly felt at home in the water; he wasn't afraid. He was treading water and actually enjoyed it. He was thinking about what his past might have been, how water might have been a part of it when he realized that Wally hadn't surfaced yet.

He instinctively gulped in air and dove under the surface of the lake toward the truck. He pulled himself in through the open door and saw Wally unconscious with his foot stuck. He frantically pulled Wally's foot out of his boot and yanked him from the truck. Using his free arm he quickly propelled them to the surface.

They were twenty-five yards from shore. J.C. grabbed Wally with the expertise of a *Baywatch Lifeguard* and had Wally beached on the shoreline in seconds. He gave Wally rescue breathing until Wally coughed violently, expelling water from his lungs.

J.C. was elated to see Wally revive. Wally continued coughing up the remaining water from his lungs. J.C. slouched onto one elbow and gave silent thanks.

"How'd I get here?" Wally asked. "My foot was—"

"Your foot was stuck in that barge you call a boot. You were trying to untie it."

Wally looked around. No one was in sight. "You . . . you saved me?"

"Yeah. I saved your sorry ass. Me. The guy who can't swim."

"How did you . . . ?"

"I just did it. I can really swim, and swim quite well I might add."

Wally's relief was evident. "You amaze me."

Chapter 33

"Paul should have called by now," J.C. whispered, not wanting the steelworkers sitting at the bar to hear.

"It's only nine-thirty. It'll take a while for him to interview Tony and find Mark," Wally said, pushing his empty cup toward J.C. "I'll have another shot of java."

"I could use another one myself, and something to eat too," J.C. ripped open a package of Oreos. "That was a long and exciting day we had yesterday."

After Wally had checked out of the hospital, they spent the remainder of Monday evening at the Port Clinton Police Station. Their statements were taken by two uniformed officers, then they were interviewed by a detective. Wally called Paul and told him what had happened. Paul was especially interested that Hawkins had mentioned the clue about the commander's son, Tony. When Wally and J.C. finally reached their hotel, it was 11:00 p.m.; they showered and went to bed. They agreed to leave at 3:00 a.m. because they were excited and couldn't sleep.

The phone rang. An arm's length away, J.C. snatched the receiver from its cradle.

"Wally, it's for you; it's Paul."

Wally yanked the phone out of J.C.'s hands. He had a serious look on his face that quickly turned to one of impatience. "I'm fine, really. Yes, the doctor gave me a clean bill of health," Wally looked at J.C., rolling his eyes. "I'm sure. I never felt better, thanks to my good ol' buddy J.C." He hesitated. "Hey, what did you find out?"

The furrows deepened between Wally's eyes. "What? I don't believe it; you've got to be shitting me."

J.C. opened his hands and nodded his head.

Wally frowned. "What about the Bravada?" he said in a low solemn voice. "Okay, talk to you then." Wally slid the phone toward J.C.; his face registered disappointment.

"What's the matter?" J.C. asked.

"The commander won't bring Tony in for questioning," Wally said.

"Why not?"

"He says there's no reason to question him."

J.C.'s eyes sparkled, as if he wanted to start investigating again. "Maybe we can talk to him."

"Not a chance. The commander has him lawyered up."

J.C. felt betrayed. He had always looked up to the commander, had always been grateful for his help in using his authority to search for his identity.

"Is this American law enforcement?" he said. "He's the police commander. He should be setting an example."

"He's protecting his kid."

"What about the chief, or the mayor?" J.C. asked. "Can't they make the commander force Tony to cooperate?"

"It's perfectly legal. We have to come up with enough evidence to compel him to talk. We have to find Mark. He's the answer to Jason's murder and your identity."

"But he told us—"

"That's called hearsay," Waly said. "Isn't worth a shit."

Wally and J.C. bowed their heads as if they were at a prayer meeting.

"If only Hawkins could talk," J.C. said. "Did they search his Bravada?"

Wally took a sip of coffee. "Nothing. Paul can get a search warrant for his house. Maybe there's some letters—"

"Yeah, there has to be something to connect Tony with Hawkins," J.C. said, brushing cookie crumbs from his shirt. "Wait a minute," he said as he flicked a crumb from his left breast pocket.

Wally looked at the reflective expression on J.C.'s face. "What?"

J.C. patted his chest. "When Hawkins mentioned Tony's name, he tapped his shirt pocket."

Wally looked puzzled.

"I guess you couldn't see what I was doing when I was attending to Hawkins; you were behind me," J.C. said. "I took a folded-up paper he was pointing to in his pocket and stuffed it in mine."

J.C.'s eyes brightened. He smiled and began gesturing with his hands. "In the heat of the moment, and trying to save his life, I completely forgot about the paper. I was concentrating on what he was trying to say."

Wally sat straight up, his hands on the table as if he was ready to stand up. "Where is it?"

"It's still in my shirt pocket. The blue one I had on yesterday. I threw it in the dirty clothes bag."

"Go get it!"

J.C. jumped out of the booth and headed for the stairs. "I'll be right back."

#

J.C. returned with the paper and tried to pry the folds apart, but the paper was still damp. They had sat around in wet clothes waiting for Wally to be checked at the hospital and during questioning at the police station. The drying process had been slowed down by the fact that the paper was folded four times and was placed in a plastic dirty clothes bag, insulating it from the air.

"Be careful," Wally said. "Don't tear it. Do you have a hair dryer?"

"No . . . but I have a microwave," J.C. said, picking up the paper. "Let's try that."

J.C. headed for the bar. Wally followed.

"What do you think, about six seconds?"

Wally shrugged.

J.C. reached for a paper plate under the bar. He placed the folded paper on the plate, put it in the oven and set the timer for six seconds.

Wally walked over and looked through the glass door of the oven. "I've heard of eating your words before," he said, "but this is ridiculous."

"We're not going to eat them. Hopefully Tony will."

The buzzer went off.

"Is it done?" Wally asked.

"Medium rare," J.C. said, as he examined the paper. "Maybe three more seconds."

"Go for it, chef."

The buzzer went off again. J.C. removed the paper and unfolded it. He glanced at the first page. "Wally, you'd better call Paul."

Chapter 34

Paul walked into the back room of Ducheck's as the clock struck eleven. "This better be good," he said. "The commander's been on my ass all morning."

He sounded tough, as if he didn't care, but he was relieved that Wally and J.C. made it back safely. He didn't need to be wrong again; he didn't need another excuse to be friends with the booze that had lost his only true friend—Gerri.

Wally and J.C. jumped up at the same time. Barb remained seated. She was off today, for the first time in ten days. She'd go back on Saturday—the midnight shift. J.C. shook the wrinkled paper at Paul.

"It's good all right," he said, "and it'll get the commander off your ass too."

"It's more than that," Wally continued, waving his hands and slobbering on his last few words. "It proves Mark Smith murdered Jason Saxberg."

J.C. explained about Hawkins dying in his arms, how Hawkins motioned to the slip of paper and how he had forgotton about it in the heat of the moment when he was trying to save Hawkins' life.

"Okay, okay," Paul said. "What's it say?"

"It says that Mark Smith murdered Jason Saxberg and you can interrogate Tony Albright," Wally answered.

Paul slumped into the booth next to Barb, shaking his head as if he couldn't believe what he was hearing. Barb put her arm around his shoulder. Wally and J.C. slid onto the bench opposite them.

"What? Tony Albright?" Paul asked. "I don't understand. What did—"

Wally interrupted. "J.C., maybe you'd better start from the beginning."

J.C. read from the paper:

> In the event of my death, this letter is to be turned over to the police. Mark Smith murdered Jason Saxberg and is trying to eliminate any witnesses. Tony Albright has information that will verify this.

Paul listened intently. He rubbed his chin as if he was thinking about his next move. He snatched the paper from J.C. and stared at it.

"What's the matter Paul? You look disappointed. This sews things up. Doesn't it?"

"This proves a lot to me, but it won't stand up in court."

Wally and J.C. looked at each other like three-year-olds who'd just found out Santa didn't exist.

Barb finally asked, "Why not?"

"First of all this declaration was typed; anyone could have typed it. Second, since Hawkins is dead, the authenticity and origin of the note can't be verified."

Wally pounded the table with his fist. "We can testify, can't we? Hawkins gave the note to us."

"It won't hold up in court," Paul said. "Any defense attorney would have it thrown out."

J.C.'s head dropped. He felt dejected. He thought the note would erase all doubts as to who murdered Jason and finally bring the killer to justice.

"What happens now? Mark has probably left town. Until we find him—"

"We have his roommate," Paul said, sliding out of the booth. "Nuggets can tell us where to find Mark."

Wally and J.C. followed Paul to the door.

"You think he'll help us?" J.C. asked.

"I'll interview him with Pastorkovich. We'll double-team him. That should work; it does on most hardened criminals."

J.C.'s spirits brightened when he heard Paul's plan. Mark Smith held the key that would unlock his identity. Maybe the answer to his heritage and past were within reach after all. J.C. and Barb watched Paul walk to his unmarked squad car, and maybe a few steps closer to the truth.

#

At headquarters, Paul found Pastorkovich at his desk looking over paperwork on a home-invasion case.

"Pastor, I could use your help with an interview."

Don Pastorkovich looked up, brushing his paperwork aside. "Yeah, sure. Who?"

"Russell Payne. He was brought in yesterday."

Pastor tilted back in his chair, his elbows slid over the armrests. "Not today, Paul."

Paul raised his eyebrows and frowned. He struck a defiant pose, hands on his hips and head tilted for battle. He glared at Pastor, waiting for an answer.

"He was released," Pastor said. "Couldn't hold him after twenty-four hours."

"Son of a bitch!" Paul turned on a heel and headed for the elevator.

The third-floor corridor was practically deserted. He brushed past the receptionist and opened the door to Commander Albright's office.

"What the hell do you want?" the commander looked up from his paperwork, his gold-plated pen in mid-air over a stack of papers.

"Russell Payne was released," Paul said. "I needed to talk to him."

The commander went back to writing. "We couldn't hold him any longer. His twenty-four hours were up. You know that."

Paul slumped into a chair in front of the commander. The gaze from his questioning eyes fell upon the mahogany desk. A photograph of the Albright family stared back at him.

"I have to find him," Paul's pleading voice echoed in the room. "He can lead us to Jason Saxberg's murderer—maybe Reverend Smith's too."

"How can this Payne boy help?" The commander stopped writing again.

"He was Mark Smith's roommate. I believe Mark murdered Jason Saxberg and I need Russell Payne to find Mark."

"Why bother with him? Put out an all points bulletin on Mark."

"I have to find Payne too. I think he was supplying information to someone other than Mark."

The commander took off his glasses and leaned forward. "Why do you suspect that?"

"I checked with the Fayetteville police. Mark was home when the reverend and Fleming were murdered—"

The commander interrupted. "So? What does that prove? You say he murdered Saxberg, right?"

"I believe he did. But there's another killer out there—the person Russell Payne was supplying information to. That person knew where J.C. Ducheck would be on both nights when attempts were made on his life. Russell is the only one who knew beside Wally and me. I believe that person's the one who murdered Reverend Smith and Fleming."

The commander sat back in his chair. "Put out A.P.B.'s on both of them then."

"Okay." Paul stood up and started walking away. "Oh, one more thing."

"What's that?"

"I'd like to talk to your son, Tony."

"That's all. You're dismissed."

#

The police sirens were loud enough to disturb General Braddock in his grave. A dark green truck sped passed Fort Necessity and the village of Farmington at a high rate of speed. In pursuit was a Uniontown police officer who'd been following it since five o'clock when the truck driver raced through a red light when leaving town. Now the truck was within fifteen miles of crossing the Maryland border.

The driver of the truck probably figured that the patrol car had radioed ahead, calling for a roadblock; the logical place to stop him would be at the Yough Dam. About a half-mile before the dam, the truck turned off onto an old township road which would eventually connect with Maryland and provide easy access to the hills and back roads of West Virginia.

What the driver didn't figure on was a large sign coming up that said the road was under construction. With only two miles to go to the border, the truck rounded a curve and swerved off the road onto the unfinished berm. The driver lost control and the truck rolled over twice before crashing through the guardrail and over a forty-foot embankment.

Minutes later, the officer reached the scene. It wasn't pretty. The driver had been ejected with enough force to completely turn his head around. Instead of watching where he was going, he would now have been able to see where he had been—that's if he'd still be alive to see. The officer pulled the wallet from the driver's back pocket and removed the photo driver's license.

#

The six o'clock news had just finished when the beer bottle hit the picture tube and it imploded. Two patrons ducked for cover; another staggered out the door. Paul had arrived a few minutes earlier to tell J.C. about Mark Smith being chased by the police and the crash that killed him.

J.C. stood behind the bar, bracing himself with his arms outstretched on the counter-top. "What the fuck am I going to do now?" he said, reaching for another bottle. "Mark Smith's the only one who knew my real identity."

Paul grabbed his arm. "Hold on. That may not be true."

J.C. slowly dropped the bottle back into the cooler. "What do you mean?" He felt stunned, almost relieved, as if a ray of hope had broken through the black cloud that had been hovering over him.

"For one thing, Jason told you he saw a red Buick drive off the night you were shot and that the same Buick tried to run him off the road. Right?"

J.C. had forgotten the details of what Jason said, only that the person who tried to kill him would know his identity.

"Yeah, I forgot about that," He said. Wrinkles of amazement on his forehead turned to doubting furrows between his eyes. "But he could have borrowed the Buick or stolen it."

"He wouldn't have stolen the same Buick twice," Paul said.

"Don't forget Nuggets," Wally said. "He was Mark's roommate."

"I was coming to that," Paul said. "We have an A.P.B. out on him. He'll show up sooner or later."

"I'd prefer sooner," J.C. said. "What about Tony? He could help us out."

Paul sighed. "He could, but the commander won't let us talk to him."

Wally bit his lip as he spoke. "Maybe he was involved in the reverend's murder."

\#

Paul's memory banks immediately placed a vision on his brain for viewing. He was back in the commander's office, looking at the commander's family photograph. The commander wasn't in uniform; he was wearing a dark blue pinstriped suit. His wife, Miriam, stood next to him dressed in an expensive-looking suit, maybe a Versace. Their sons, Tony and Philip were seated in front of them.

"I just remembered something," Paul said. "Philip, Tony's younger brother—he's been institutionalized since his early teens. He had a nervous breakdown or something."

"You think there's a connection?" Wally asked.

"I remember Philip got sick about the same time that the rifle team was flourishing."

"Do you think the reverend was responsible for sending Philip over the edge?" J.C. asked. "You think Tony found out about it?"

"Could be," Paul said. "I need to have a talk with Harrold Stuhl and Jim Michaels. That'll give me a clearer picture. And then there's Troy Butterfield; he might know something."

J.C. seemed energized. "He could have killed Fleming too. He was mixed up in drugs with Hawkins and Mark."

"Maybe the commander wasn't just protecting his son," Wally said. "Maybe he was covering for the drug trade, too."

Paul shook his head. "That's too far-fetched. One thing at a time. Finding Nuggets or Russell Payne or whatever he calls himself is our main concern."

"How long will that take," J.C. asked.

"I sent his fingerprints in about ten days ago. I should be hearing from A.F.I.S. soon. We'll go from there."

The sound of electric arcing and puffs of smoke were issuing from the TV when Wally and Paul left.

Chapter 35

Black Thursday was the term that came to mind as Paul looked at the body in the garbage heap. A refuse worker had discovered the corpse at the West end Garbage Dump and flagged down a patrolman who immediately notified headquarters. Paul got the assignment.

Staring at the body of Russell Payne, a.k.a. Nuggets, Paul felt his optimism slowly drain away. Any chance he had of solving the murders of Reverend Smith and Jason Saxberg could be as dead as Nuggets.

This can't be happening, he thought. Every turn I make is blocked, like someone's looking over my shoulder. What am I going to tell J.C.?

Except for the commander's son Tony, Paul figured Nuggets/Payne was his last hope of solving the murders.

Two men from the ME's office loaded Nuggets' body on a gurney, slid it into the waiting meat wagon and drove away, while Paul watched disheartened from his car. He knew that Tony was the key to everything. Paul had to find a way to convince him to come forward and let him know that protecting his father's reputation wasn't in his, or his father's, best interests.

229

Maybe he could pressure Tony by threatening to expose his drug activity. Those who had known the most about his drug connections were dead. Fleming was found in a garbage bag in the park but there were others. Jimmy Restivo and Leslie Carter both knew Fleming. They might supply some information about his connection with Tony. Katie McClure might prove useful with information on Mark Smith. Then there was the rifle team. A few of those kids knew about Hawkins' connection to Tony.

Paul felt somewhat relieved that his planning was starting to make some sense to him. But what if no one cooperated? What if he couldn't get close enough to Tony to talk to him? Could he threaten him anyway? What would the commander do? Paul thought about going over his head, but breaking the chain of command on unproven theories would only make him look silly and discredit any future attempts to solve Reverend Smith's murder.

Paul stopped for a red light at the corner of Mayhew and McKee. He looked up the street at a gray stuccoed house and recognized it as Councilman Martinet's. Then it hit him. He might be able to persuade the commander into letting him talk to Tony. Martinet had told Paul about Chief Murdock's visit to Julius Butterfield's house and that Murdock found out Julius was blackmailing the reverend about indiscretions with Julius' son Troy. Maybe the commander knew about it. Maybe he was involved in a cover-up. If that was true, and Paul confronted the commander with the information, the commander would have to cooperate with him. That was something he'd have to explore after lunch.

#

The walk to Chief Tressler's office didn't take long. The information Paul had received after lunch turned black Thursday a lot brighter.

Paul had been sitting at his desk mulling over various ways to approach the commander about his cooperation when the office secretary dropped the results of Russell Payne's fingerprints on his desk. Paul ripped open the manila envelope and discovered that, in fact, Russell Payne was Nuggets' true name. A yellow sheet accompanied the fingerprint results. Payne had various arrests for drug use, pandering and breaking and entering. He had been honorably discharged from the 82nd Airborne Division three months before he showed up at Ducheck's. His military record was clean.

As far as Paul knew, the only connection Payne had in all this was to Mark, and Mark was dead. Another dead end. He was considering again how to approach the commander when he noticed that another sheet was stuck to Russell Payne's arrest record and fingerprint results. He worked the sheet loose and stared. It was J.C.'s fingerprint results.

The door to the chief's office was open, so Paul walked in.

"You look anxious," Tressler said. Paul knew the chief didn't like people barging in, uninvited, let alone jumping the chain of command.

"I think this will explain things, sir," Paul placed J.C.'s fingerprint sheet on the desk in front of him.

Chief Tressler wrapped the stems of his spectacles around his ears and picked up the paper to read.

"Well, I'll be dammed." He picked up the phone and punched a button on the cradle. "Lieutenant, get the duty sergeant and escort Commander Albright to my office."

"This is a private party now." After ushering Wally and Councilman inside, Ted Martinet Paul flipped the two-sided sign on the door from open to closed. Barb was already inside, seated at a table. Paul had called her from the office before he left, asking her to meet him at the bar. Barb joined them in front of a bewildered J.C. Paul locked the door before joining them.

"Hell's goin' on?" J.C. was washing glasses. He placed his wet hands on his hips. "What's the occasion?"

"We've got two things to celebrate," Councilman Martinet said. "Paul, you want to go first?"

J.C. and Barb shifted their attention toward Paul.

"Well?" Wally asked.

"Give us a drink first," Paul said. "What kind of celebration is this without a drink?"

There was a knock at the door.

"I'll get it," Martinet said, walking back to unlock it. Gerri stood there, smiling shyly. Martinet ushered her inside to everyone's surprise.

Paul was speechless, but happy.

"I'll have a beer," Gerri said, surprising him even more.

Paul had trouble putting a sentence together. "Gerri . . . What . . . Why?"

"Ted explained what happened and how you've . . ." She lowered her head in an apologetic manner. "And that you've . . ."

Paul interrupted. "I'm glad you're here." He wrapped his arm around her shoulder and walked her to the bar.

J.C. set up the bar, as the eager "customers" smiled in anticipation of what Paul was about to say—the reason he'd brought them all together.

Paul smiled at Gerri, took a long draw on his I.C. Light, and smacked his lips in approval. "First thing is that the reverend's murder has been solved. Second, and more important, is we now know that the reverend's son, Mark, murdered Jason Saxberg."

J.C.'s face lit up.

"All right! Great!" J.C. said. "When did you find out about the reverend's murder? Who did it? Who killed him? Tony?"

"No, it was Tony's father, Commander Albright," Paul said.

J.C. stepped backward, openedmouthed. He sucked in his breath as if cooling hot food. "The commander? But why? He was trying to help me. He wouldn't—"

Paul interrupted. "The commander found out from his son, Tony, why Philip had a breakdown. It was because Reverend Smith had been molesting him for years. The commander wanted revenge. He wanted to get back at the reverend's family first by killing Smith and then making it look like Matthew—the reverend's son—had killed his father. The next part of the commander's plan was to get Mark convicted of Jason Saxberg's murder."

"So Fleming and Nuggets worked for the commander?"

"That's right, J.C."

J.C. thought for a minute. "That's why Fleming suddenly changed his mind and wanted to meet with us. He laid the false trail to Mark."

"Correct," Paul said, "and the commander murdered Fleming and Nuggets too. He covered for himself very well."

"Except for two little things," Wally said.

"What's that?" J.C. asked. "And who tried to kill me? The commander wouldn't have any reason to kill me."

Paul nodded. "We'll get to that. Tell him Wally."

"Let's get back to the things that the commander didn't account for. First, Paul's determination," Wally hoisted his beer in a salute to Paul. The others clinked their bottles together. Gerri raised her bottle to Paul's. The two gazed into each other's eyes like teen-agers as they drank the toast.

"And second," Wally raised his beer in J.C.'s direction, "to J.C.'s fingerprints and Councilman Martinet's inquiry."

J.C. couldn't believe what he'd just heard. "My fingerprints? The commander—"

"The commander never sent them in," Wally explained. "He lied to you. He didn't want you to discover your identity. When he thought you were getting close and he had the opportunity, he tried to kill you."

J.C. was shocked. He slumped on a stool. "But why? Why

wouldn't he want me to find my identity? What difference did it make to him?"

Councilman Martinet spoke up. "He had a million reasons for not wanting you to discover who you are. You stood to inherit half a million dollars from your grandfather."

J.C.'s and Barbs eyes met simultaneously. J.C. saw the same surprise reflected back at him. Knowing that his identity was about to be revealed made his stomach to churn with a mixture of joy and uncertainty.

"Who am I?" J.C. asked, jumping off the stool, his eyes pleading for an answer. What's my name?"

Barb put her glass down with a shaky hand. She reached over to grip J.C.'s arm.

Wally smiled and hesitated an instant before speaking. "Jeffrey. You're Jeffrey Albright."

"Albright!"

"You're the commander's nephew," Martinet said. "You were a Marine Corps corporal at Kosovo. You were with the Twenty-Sixth Expeditionary Unit on June the twenty-fifth, nineteen ninety-nine, when it came under small arms fire near the town of Gnjilane. That's where your prior gunshot came from. You were wounded and flown to Ramstein Air Force Base in Germany, then driven to Landstuhl Regional Medical Center. You spent a total of two months recuperating from your wound, before receiving orders to return stateside for reassignment. Since you weren't with your unit, you flew commercial airlines. Apparently, for some unknown reason, you switched tickets with another G I and took a later flight. The flight you should have been on went in the drink; everyone was lost. Your name was on the manifest."

"The plane you'd taken instead arrived at Kennedy shortly before the news about the downed plane was released; it was considered late or diverted due to a storm. You flew on to Pittsburgh and called your uncle, your only living relative, who agreed to pick you up. By then, word had spread about the plane crashing, the flight you passed up. You told your uncle about it on the way to his house. That's when he shot you."

"My own uncle shot me?" J.C.'s eyes saddened.

"He shot you because your grandfather, who had passed away when you were in Kosovo, left a million dollars to his two remaining heirs," Martinet said. "The commander stood to collect all of it with you out of the picture. With your name on the crashed plane's manifest, you were already considered dead."

J.C.'s rage surfaced. He'd accumulated years of hatred for the person who had shot him and left him for dead that day in the ravine, traumatizing him so badly that he'd blocked out his own identity and adopted a new personality.

"Is he the one who cut my brake line and tried to shoot me that night coming back from the Community College?"

"One and the same," Paul said. "He probably tried to kill Jason too. Mark didn't plan to kill Jason. He did it on the spur of the moment, I believe. The commander's work was premeditated. He knew exactly what he was doing. He wanted to get rid of a witness—if you had regained your memory, you could have put him in jail."

J.C. lowered his head. "I guess remorse finally caused him to confess."

"No," Paul said. "He made a full confession to avoid the death penalty."

J.C. couldn't hold back the tears; he wept openly. Barb jumped up from her stool and ran to him with open arms. They embraced, both crying.

Wally patted J.C. on the back. "You know who you are now," he said. "You know your name."

J.C. looked at Barb and then at the others. "Yeah," he said. "I know who I am. I've known for a long time. My name's J.C. Ducheck."

Gerri wrapped her arm around Paul's waist. "I know who you are too. You're the man I love." They left, leaving the others to celebrate.

Printed in the United States
18921LVS00002B/6